LOVE IN THE LIMELIGHT

LOVE IN THE LIMELIGHT

by

Ashley Moore

2021

LOVE IN THE LIMELIGHT

ISBN 13: 978-1-63679-051-0

This Trade Paperback Original Is Published By
Bold Strokes Books, Inc.
P.O. Box 249
Valley Falls, NY 12185

First Edition: September 2021

CREDITS
Editors: Jenny Harmon and Cindy Cresap
Production Design: Susan Ramundo
Cover Design By Tammy Seidick

Acknowledgments

I started writing this book because I was unemployed, and between job hunts, I didn't have anything else to do. So, I wrote. I wrote a lot. I wrote furiously. I have never written so much in such a short period of time. There were many people who supported me as I was writing this novel. My mom, who supported my ambition to write even though my love of writing baffled her. My girlfriend, Nike, who I met thanks to my writing and who told me that what I was doing was worthwhile. My best friend, ak, who reads everything I write and always has. Clio, who pushed me to make this story much better than it would have been without her help. Kyla and Elliott, who gave me invaluable feedback on the last draft before I submitted this for publishing. Thanks also to my editor, Jennifer Harmon, who made this book much better than I could have done alone and who made the process as painless as possible, and to everyone at Bold Strokes Books who supported me in this endeavor. Finally, thank you to everyone who picks up this book and reads it. I hope you enjoy it.

Dedication

For my mom, my unwavering support system

CHAPTER ONE

Present Day

"Lift your face just a bit." Light fingertips tilted Marion's face upward to a better angle for Roxanne to do her work. Marion knew the routine by now. She closed her eyes as cool fingers smoothed primer into her skin. Taking a deep breath, she tried to relax into it. Roxanne had been her makeup artist for years, working with her on film after film, and like tonight, for the occasional event she couldn't gracefully avoid. She was one of the few people Marion would allow into the sanctuary of her home.

"This always feels a bit ridiculous, putting on evening wear in the afternoon." Marion sighed, her British accent contrasting with Roxanne's flat, Southern Californian one.

"Time zones are a bitch," Roxanne agreed. "But I don't think you'd be able to convince them to start the ceremony any later."

"No, I wouldn't think so." Marion's hair was already up, and her dress hung on the door to her closet, ready to be put on as soon as her makeup was finished.

Roxanne moved on to her eyes. Eyeshadow and then eyeliner in quick, efficient strokes. Marion kept her eyes open after Roxanne finished putting pomade in her eyebrows to keep them tidy. So much work, so much effort. She might have enjoyed it once, all the attention, all the care directed entirely on making her presentable, but the excitement had worn off years ago.

She looked at herself as Roxanne started to apply various layers of corrector and concealer until she looked like a better, more perfect version of herself. It was a false promise though. What would the audiences think if they knew how much she didn't want to attend the ceremony tonight? Surely, the Academy Awards had to be the height of the Hollywood social calendar. Didn't everyone want a ticket? Marion wanted nothing more than to stay home and ignore the awards altogether. She could find out who won in the next day's paper.

The doorbell rang.

Marion could hear the front door open, then close again. A minute later, Barbara, her assistant, entered the room, a bouquet of violets in her hands. Roxanne paused as Marion turned.

Marion sucked in a breath.

"One day you're going to tell me who sends you these mystery flowers." Barbara stopped in the doorway. "Where would you like them?"

Marion should have expected the flower delivery, but she hadn't. Handing out an award hardly seemed to warrant the attention. But they showed up without fail anyway.

"On the vanity is fine." Marion swallowed against the thickness in her throat.

"Of course." Barbara placed the flowers to one side of the vanity. "Your car should be here in a bit. I'll let you know."

"Thank you." Marion turned back toward Roxanne as Barbara left the room.

Following the concealer, Roxanne moved on to brushing foundation over Marion's face. Marion closed her eyes again. She imagined she could feel every bristle of the brush against her skin, each stroke putting another layer between her and everyone who would look at her that night. Contour, highlighter, blush, then powder to set it all. More layers. More distance.

The lips came next. Hers were a bit thin, but you'd never know it once Roxanne finished with them. Movie magic even when she wasn't on the set of a film. Lip liner and lipstick, more powder, more armor.

"Look up." Marion lifted her eyes to the ceiling as Roxanne put mascara on her lower lashes. Her stylist had already come and gone, trusting her to complete her ensemble to the required specifications on her own. She would look flawless when she presented the best actor award later that evening. She would need to with all of the cameras that would be focused on her. On a night like tonight, they wouldn't leave her alone. Her dress, her jewelry, her makeup, it would all be fair game, and as much as it annoyed her, she had an image to maintain.

"There you go," Roxanne said as she put the mascara wand away and finished putting on her false lashes. "You're going to cut a striking figure in all that black." She nodded toward the dress.

Marion glanced at herself in the mirror. She supposed Roxanne was correct. "Yes, well, you know I'm not one for experimenting. Or winding up on *worst dressed* lists." She reached out for a box on the vanity and opened it, revealing a diamond necklace. It sparkled almost to excess, but her stylist had said it was vital to the ensemble, so Marion would wear it.

"I don't think you need to worry about that." Roxanne started packing her things away. "Is your joke any good?"

"Hmm?" Marion pulled her gaze away from the necklace. "Oh, no. It's dreadful." She rolled her eyes. "But what can you expect, really? Jokes written by committee are bound to be lackluster." She removed the necklace from the box and fastened it around her neck. "But I'll tell it with great gusto and no one will know how I really feel," she said as if imparting a secret.

Roxanne chuckled. "I won't tell." She winked.

"I appreciate your discretion," Marion said.

They both looked in the mirror at Marion's reflection. For a moment, Marion wondered what Roxanne saw. Probably just a job well done.

"Well, I'm finished here." Roxanne put away the last of her things, picked up her bag, and slung the strap over her shoulder.

"Thank you." Marion nodded and Roxanne showed herself out. Her eyes fell back down onto her reflection, checking it one more time.

She looked at the bouquet of violets sitting on the edge of her vanity. She lightly shook her head and focused on her task for the night.

She would run the gauntlet of press on the red carpet and put up with insipid comments about her dress. She would feign interest in the ceremony just in case any of the cameras that panned across the audience came to rest on her. She would go on stage, make an ill-thought-out joke that she did not write about being the most successful spinster in Hollywood, and then she would present the Best

Actor award to an already-anointed pretentious prick for his work on the latest navel-gazing, bullshit film she had wanted to walk out of in the first thirty minutes. Once that was finished, she just had to survive the innumerable parties and she could put the entire affair behind her for another year.

❖

Marion stood at the edge of the stage, envelope resting lightly in her hands. She resisted the urge to fidget with it. Someone would want it later as a keepsake and she didn't want to bend the edges. A woman stood next to her holding the statuette. Marion spared her a glance. Young and blandly pretty in her evening wear. She would blend into the background perfectly. Her only job requirement. Marion ran through her joke in her head once again. She wouldn't want to flub it in front of the world.

She remembered the prior year. Oscar number three sat in her office at home. It would be collecting dust if she didn't have someone to come in and clean on a regular basis. She didn't pay it any mind. She cared more about what came next. But she didn't have a project planned at the moment, wasn't sure what the future would look like. Nothing had seemed appealing lately. Everything was focus-grouped to death now. No one was taking risks. Not of the sort she was interested in at this point in her career. She'd put in her time taking the expected parts, being the grand doyenne of serious acting for what felt like ages. She wanted to do new things, things that pushed her, things that took her out of her comfort zone. Maybe she'd take some time off, go someplace tropical, or go back to London for a bit.

Marion was pulled from her thoughts as her name was announced through the theater. She put on a convincing smile and stepped onto the stage. Time to get this over with.

❖

The ceremony was finished, the awards given out, and Marion's night was that much closer to being over. Only the parties remained. This was the second one she had attended that night. She stared out at the valley below her, a chaotic sea of lights and palm trees. Nothing interesting. Nothing special. It wasn't London, but she had gotten used to it over the years. At some point, it had even become home. The party flowed on behind her, a cacophony of sound and movement filled with people celebrating their wins and commiserating over their losses, all far more inebriated than Marion cared to be.

Marion heard a shriek and turned to see a young blond woman, possibly one of the nominees from earlier, throwing her arms around another bright young thing. They were supposed to be the future of Hollywood. Marion could barely remember their names.

She sighed. Her attendance at this particular party was a necessary evil, born of politics and politeness. Movie stars and other hangers-on crammed into every corner of the room, but she didn't care to interact with any of them. Three Academy Awards and the parties got no less tedious.

Subtly pulling her phone out of her bag, Marion checked the time. Three fifteen a.m. She sipped her champagne as she looked toward the exit. Surely, she had subjected herself to this torture long enough. She set her glass on a side table and prepared to leave only to feel a light touch at her elbow.

Turning, Marion found Margaret at her side. Short and round, Margaret looked nothing like your stereotypical Hollywood agent. The straitlaced gray bob and mild expression gave her the appearance of a kindly teacher, but Marion knew appearances could be deceiving and that a shrewd mind lurked behind grandmotherly glasses.

"I know you want to be going, so I won't keep you for too long." Margaret's eyes alighted on the crowd around them and she looked far more jovial than Marion felt. "But you need to come by my office tomorrow. Let's say two o'clock? Gwen's asking for a favor and I want to talk it over with you."

"What's to talk over? If Gwen needs something, you know I'm happy to help." Gwen Harrington had given Marion her first big break. Marion had a long memory, and if there was any way she could repay the aging movie star, she would do it.

"You don't even know what she's asking for. At least glance over the script before you agree." Margaret smiled up at Marion then looked toward the door. "I know you're anxious to get home, so I'll leave you to it. Just remember: my office, tomorrow afternoon, two o'clock sharp." Margaret squeezed Marion's forearm and rejoined the crowd.

Marion was still watching Margaret when someone stumbled into her side. Marion automatically reached out to steady whoever it was. The shrieking woman from earlier looked up at her in shock.

"God, I'm so sorry." She held onto Marion for another moment as she got her balance. "I—"

"Are you all right?" Marion held her hands out as if the woman might fall over again.

"I…yeah, I'm—" the woman shook her head as she looked up at her. Marion could see the moment she was recognized. "Damn." There was awe in the woman's voice. "You…you're gorgeous. I mean, I knew that, I just didn't… know."

The woman just blinked up at Marion as if processing her presence. She finally shook herself out of her reverie. "Can I get you a drink? You need a drink. You don't have one." She swayed on her feet. "Or I could brave the dessert table for you. The tiny cakes are amazing."

"That won't be necessary," Marion said. Something about the questions amused her though and she smiled.

"I'd be happy to do it," the woman said, leaning into Marion's personal space.

Marion blinked. She looked down at the woman and caught the look in her eyes. She had seen that look before. It had been years and years, but the woman's eyes looked so familiar. Familiar enough that Marion automatically wanted to take care of her. She took a small step back.

"I was just making my way out, but thank you." Marion adjusted her grip on her clutch.

"Ah, well." The woman smiled as she shook her head. "I had to give it a shot. I've had a crush on you since forever. You're just amazing. Like, those cheekbones. How did you get those cheekbones?" She closed her eyes as a blush colored her skin. "And I shouldn't have said that. I'm going to regret saying that."

Marion couldn't stop herself from laughing. Whatever part of her had remained guarded crumbled at the sound of the girl's impulsive, slurred sincerity. "I'm significantly too old for you," she said gently. "But you look like you might need some help to your car."

"Yeah, that'd be…" The woman swallowed. "That'd be awesome."

That settled it. She would walk the girl to her car, good deed done for the day, and then go home.

❖

Darkness stretched out in front of Marion as she let herself into her house. She had forgotten to leave on a light, but she could find her way around in the dark well enough. She slipped off her heels and pressed her feet onto the cold tile, sighing with relief. She left them by the door to be collected in the morning.

She started pulling the pins from her hair as she walked toward her bedroom, collecting them in one hand as her hair came to rest around her shoulders. She tossed the pins onto her vanity then was brought up short by the shadow of the violets still sitting there. This time, she sighed deeply as she sank into her chair. She finished taking her hair down and ran her fingers through it to check for any tangles, then looked at her reflection again.

Nearly fifty and here she was. There were crow's feet around her eyes and lines across her forehead and she refused to do anything about either. Other actors might be willing to alter their appearance in a futile attempt to maintain relevance, but she refused to.

She brushed her fingers over the soft petals of the flowers. They would be dead in a few days and then the reminder would be gone. Until then, she'd let the soft perfume fill her room.

❖

1997

Marion sighed. She and Tabitha had already twisted their way through the house that hosted the party they were attending that night and now the patio lay in front of them. Something insipid by the Backstreet Boys pumped through the speakers. Tabitha's fingers dug into her arm where she pulled Marion through the crowd.

She craned her neck to look around the patio. Tabitha had only recently started letting her come to these parties, finally convinced that she could trust Marion out of her sight for more than five minutes. Marion relished her freedom.

"Go mingle, girl," Tabitha hissed in her ear before turning her loose. "I have too much to do tonight to babysit you. I expect you to be on your best behavior. Go look pretty and don't offend anyone."

"Of course." Marion nodded. Her arm ached, but she already knew that she wasn't going to listen to Tabitha's instructions. Oh, she supposed she would look pretty enough. That didn't involve any active participation on her part, but there was a bar in the corner and it likely had a decent bottle of scotch. Avoiding people was the easiest way to *not offend* anyone. One night off wouldn't destroy her career.

Tabitha gave her a stern look, as if she had read Marion's mind. Sometimes Marion wondered whether she could. "If I catch you fooling around, you won't like the consequences."

Marion swallowed but met Tabitha's eyes. "I know."

"Good." Tabitha held Marion's eyes for another moment before she turned around and faded into the crowd. Now that she was gone, Marion would do her best not to attract Tabitha's attention.

She made her way to the bar and slipped onto a barstool. A quick conversation with the bartender later and she had a tumbler sitting in front of her.

Keeping Tabitha happy was generally at the top of Marion's to-do list. It had been since she was a child. Her parents had abandoned her to the agent's care as soon as they'd hired her. Tabitha had done more to raise her than her parents had, and it was hard to shrug off her influence and expectations. Tabitha still treated her like the unruly teen she had never had the luxury of being, too ensnared by the expectations of producers and directors and costars, and more importantly, of Tabitha herself. If Tabitha wanted, she could snap her fingers and Marion's career would be over. She would be sent back to London, to her parents, in disgrace, and never work again. She would have nothing.

Still, Marion was feeling reckless that night. Something about the oppressive heat made her rebellious. She wanted to leave. She wanted to take the car and go to the quiet little coffee shop by her apartment where she could have a cup of tea and no one would bother her. Never mind that they were likely closed for the day. Still, she wondered how long her temporary freedom would last. Probably not as long as she'd like before she was pressed into a conversation with someone she didn't care about, her agent looming over her shoulder to make sure she smiled prettily and played nice.

She looked up at the patio reflected in the mirror behind the bar. Someone Marion didn't recognize was splashing in the shallow end of the pool with the skirt of her party dress fisted in her hand to keep it from getting wet. What would it feel like to jump into a pool in a party dress? She hadn't the faintest idea how to be that impulsive.

Other people milled about with their own cocktails in their hands, making deals and casting movies. She was so caught up in the spectacle of the woman in the pool that she didn't notice the person sliding next to her until she started speaking.

"What are you drinking tonight?" the woman asked. Marion started, and then rolled her eyes. How original. Half the men in Hollywood had tried the same line on her and it hadn't gotten them anywhere.

"Macallan. Why? Are you the bartender?" Marion replied. Maybe her curtness would be enough to make the woman go away. So much for playing nice. She had no interest in polite conversation. No. She simply wanted to leave. Despite the rising moon, sweat still beaded on her skin. She hated these parties.

"Not the bartender, no. Just curious. I, myself, am having a lovely *blanc de blanc*, but I could easily be persuaded to switch to scotch." Marion looked at the woman through the mirror. Their eyes met. Well then. Jess Carmichael. The current darling of the pop scene. Layered blond hair and too much enthusiasm for someone so small—the kind who would be described as *petite* and *bubbly* by the same tabloids that made snarky reference to Marion's *gangly* and *austere* frame.

It was an odd party for Jess to be attending, full of Hollywood moguls, and not part of LA's music scene. Why she wanted to talk to Marion was equally unclear.

"I don't persuade people to drink. And I don't invite people I don't know to drink with me." Marion deadened her tone and attempted to regard her scotch with a bored air. She didn't know how to be any more dismissive without outright telling Jess to leave. She had no desire to be a conversation placeholder for out-of-place pop stars.

"Jessica. I insist." Jess thrust her hand out along the bar in front of Marion. Marion looked at it disdainfully but took it out of politeness anyway. Tattoos shifted on Jess's skin as she moved her muscles. Shapes Marion couldn't decipher, and words she couldn't read, not in the low light. She found herself wanting to know just what the tattoos said, but there was no polite way to ask and no way for them to step into the light without Tabitha noticing them.

"Yes. I know. Your music is…not terrible."

"Why do I get the feeling that's high praise coming from you?" Jess cocked her head to the side as she smiled at Marion. Marion finally turned to actually look at Jess. It was a smile that held secrets. Jess signaled the bartender.

"Make of it what you will." She caught Jess's eyes. Jess didn't look away.

"Then I'll take the compliment." Jess really was as relentlessly positive as her music. The bartender placed two tumblers of scotch in front of them and Marion automatically accepted the drink. "The last movie you were in, where you were the teacher, it wasn't half bad."

That got Marion's attention. Jess might be cheerful, but she had some bite as well. That performance had won her an Oscar and had most people falling over themselves to tell her how wonderful it was, whether or not they had seen the film.

"You've made your point." Marion inclined her head. She took a sip of her drink and watched Jess do the same. Jess coughed lightly. Marion wasn't surprised. Jess didn't look like a scotch drinker. Marion raised an eyebrow.

Jess smiled sheepishly. "I'm not used to such strong drinks anymore. And when I was, I wasn't drinking anything so nice."

"I suppose the cocaine musicians are known for doing it much smoother." Marion smirked for just a second.

"Cocaine is so 1980s," Jess replied. "It's all MDMA now. Though you," Jess looked her up and down and Marion forced herself not to shiver, "seem more like the opium den type. Somewhere with silk curtains and fainting couches."

Marion hadn't expected Jess to tease her back. Jess looked up at her through her eyelashes, lips quirked in a crooked smile. Were they flirting? Marion wasn't sure. She wasn't out, and as far as she knew, there weren't any rumors going around to that effect. She'd never heard anything about Jess being interested in women, but this felt like more than a simple conversation. She thought hard about her response. She couldn't say anything overt, couldn't say anything that would attract attention. She could make out Tabitha on the patio, no doubt trying to land her another ingénue part.

"It's a rare indulgence." She took her own time with a frank appraisal of Jess, subtle enough that no one else would notice, but hopefully enough to let Jess know she might be interested. Jess's smile told her the message had been received.

"And an expensive one." Jess reached out and ran a fingertip down the outside of Marion's forearm. This time, Marion did shiver. Jess's smile turned into a smirk. If this was going where Marion thought it was, she was ready to move things along. She needed to move things along if she didn't want Tabitha to see. Marion swallowed the rest of her scotch, then took Jess's and finished that too. Jess laughed in delight.

Marion leaned into Jess's space. "I believe this is the point when you invite me back to your place for the next drink," she whispered. It wouldn't do to be too loud. Marion could see at least three people willing to sell tidbits about her to the gossip columns in a heartbeat. If there were any rumors, Tabitha would be the first to hear them, and she would come down on Marion with a fury Marion didn't want to experience. "I, of course, demur, you charmingly insist, and I acquiesce. Do I have it right or shall I check my script?"

Jess laughed louder this time. She leaned into Marion's space and when she responded, her voice was just as low. "I don't know. It seems you're the one who just did the inviting." Well, if that's how Jess wanted to see it, she wouldn't object. Unless she had been wrong about Jess's intentions after all.

"Perhaps I did," Marion allowed as she raised an eyebrow and stood. How would Jess respond now?

Jess licked her lips. "Well, if you did, I would say I would love to have that drink with you someplace more private, and if my apartment happens to be closer, I do have a lovely bottle of rosé I can open." They were on the same page then.

"We can go out the side gate." Marion held an arm out to let Jess precede her.

Jess nodded and started walking toward the gate. If they could get out quickly, Tabitha would be none the wiser.

Chapter Two

Present Day

Marion walked into the glass-walled building that housed Margaret's office. Her heels clicked against the marble floors, cutting through the subdued atmosphere. It seemed the entire town was suffering the same collective hangover and only Marion dared disrupt the hush. She reached Margaret's outer office and presented herself to Margaret's assistant at precisely two p.m. The assistant waved her straight through.

"My presence, as requested," Marion said as Margaret looked up from her desk. More floor to ceiling windows stretched out behind her, tinted to keep out the glare and the heat. She crossed the office and took a seat in one of the leather guest chairs that sat in front of the desk. The office was almost as familiar as her own home in Hollywood after so many years as Margaret's client.

"Ah, yes." Margaret shuffled some papers around on her cluttered desk and found the script she was looking for. She held it out for Marion. "Gwen wants you to give it a look and see if you're interested. It's a small studio, and they can't really afford you, but I know how you feel about Gwen, and she's signed on as an executive producer." Margaret shrugged. "I told her you'd give it a look, but I didn't make any promises."

Marion raised her eyebrows as she took the script and started skimming it. "A musical?" Her eyebrows rose even farther up her forehead. She'd never done a musical, never even considered doing one. She had said she wanted to do something new. Singing. Singing would be new.

"An animated adaptation of a series of beloved children's books. *Petunia's Potion.* Magic and witches and that sort of thing."

"Yes, I've read them," Marion broke in. She'd loved them as a young teenager, loved getting lost in the fantastical world when the stress placed on her to be the perfect actor got to be too much. Gwen had been the one who introduced her to the series to begin with, slipping her each book in succession while they worked together, along with the occasional piece of chocolate she could nibble on covertly away from her former agent's hawkish gaze.

She had forgotten all about the experience, but now she remembered it fondly as she skimmed through the parts of the script that had been tabbed for her.

"Gwen thought the part of the stern headmistress might suit you. She's primarily there to put the brakes on the main character's antics, keep her from blasting her own head off with her magic, that sort of thing." Margaret's eyes sparkled.

"I remember that from the books. What aren't you telling me?" Marion knew there had to be something to put that look in Margaret's eyes.

"Well, they've added a brief subplot with the headmistress of a rival school. It's all subtext, but if you look at it the right way, the two characters practically fall in love on screen."

"Headmistress?" Marion didn't remember that from the books.

"Well, like I said, it's all subtext." Margaret smiled knowingly. "But you are the master of subtext. The material is there if you want to play it that way."

Marion huffed. "Just because I'm a lesbian doesn't mean all of my characters have to be. This is exactly why I keep my private life private."

"Marion, dear, none of your characters have been lesbians. And yet you can't seem to help yourself. You can't stop people from speculating about your private life," Margaret said, shaking her head.

"I might not be able to stop them, but that doesn't mean I need to encourage them either. I don't want people speculating about what I do off screen. I had enough of that when Tabitha was making me date those horrible, self-serving men in my twenties. If I never see myself on the cover of a tabloid again, it will be too soon." Marion grumbled, glaring at Margaret, who was giving Marion her patented long-suffering look. "I will not be made a spectacle of."

Margaret looked at Marion over the top of her glasses.

"You know, if you just stopped hiding, you wouldn't have to worry so much about whatever covert signals you think you might be giving off."

Marion blanched. "We've had this discussion before. We needn't have it again. My private life is private. Whatever plans you have for my public coming out, shelve them." It was a topic she and Margaret had discussed many times, and each time, Marion had balked. While in her late twenties,

Tabitha had trotted her out like a show pony, determined to prove Marion's straightness to whomever might be speculating otherwise. Tabitha's obsession and public pressure had nearly led to what would have been a disaster of a marriage. Now that Tabitha no longer had a hold on her, ever since she had been freed to choose how she conducted her own life, she guarded her privacy fiercely. She wouldn't be pressured into giving it up. Not for Margaret, not for her fans' or the tabloids' endless desire to know more about her private life, not for anything.

Margaret shook her head. "All right. I'll drop it. And technically, the two headmistresses only have a few scenes together, and they spend most of them at odds. Richard could decide on a million different ways to have them interact."

"Richard?"

"Thompson. He's signed on to direct."

Marion knew the name but didn't know much about the man beyond that he was British too, by way of Jamaica, slightly scatterbrained, and generally well liked.

Marion looked down at the script once again, giving it more careful consideration this time. The room descended into silence as she turned pages. "It doesn't look horrible. And it's only a few days of work," she said. She owed Gwen and she had loved the books as a child. There was little that would truly harm her career. Even if the movie flopped, it could simply be written off as something she'd done for the nostalgia. She made up her mind.

"Work out the details with the studio. Don't play hardball when it comes to pay."

"Excellent." Margaret smiled brightly. "Gwen will be thrilled." She clapped her hands together.

Marion started to take her leave only to have Margaret continue, "Have you met Jess Carmichael? She's doing the music, and I think they've cast her as the rival headmistress."

The name stopped Marion short. "Jess Carmichael?" She slowly unfolded to her full height. "We've met, yes. Briefly." Marion's throat worked as it suddenly felt impossible to swallow. "It'll be good to see her again. Now, if you'll excuse me."

She tried not to stagger toward the door, but she wasn't sure she succeeded. The air in Margaret's office was suddenly too close, nearly suffocating her. She pushed out into the outer office and didn't stop her flight until she was safely in the bathroom.

Hand against her stomach, she finally managed a deep breath. She stepped to the sink and turned on the water, letting it run over her wrists. She splashed some on her face then grabbed a paper towel to blot the water away. Jessica. She had spent years trying to avoid her, futile as it might have been. Jessica hadn't gotten a hundred million Twitter followers by avoiding the limelight.

Twenty-four years later and Marion still hadn't managed to truly banish Jess from her awareness, but she had gotten close. She no longer flinched when she heard Jess's music on the radio. She no longer looked over her shoulder every time she visited London.

Now, Jess would be back in her life. There would be no way to ignore her presence.

With another swipe of the paper towel, and a long look in the mirror, Marion gathered herself and left the bathroom. There were things she needed to take care of that day. The hangovers of everyone in the city be damned.

❖

1997

Slipping through the side gate, Marion looked furtively around the edge of the hedges that ringed the mansion where the party was taking place. She needed to make sure Tabitha wasn't anywhere in sight. One glimpse of Marion trying to sneak out of the party and the promise of the night would be destroyed.

"What are we hiding from?" Jess whispered in Marion's ear, a teasing smile in her voice.

"What?" Marion shook her head and looked over her shoulder to find Jess.

"I said." Jess reached for Marion's face and pulled her down into a quick kiss. Marion's breath caught in her chest. She couldn't breathe. She couldn't think. All she could think about was Jess's lips against her own. Just as quickly as it started, the kiss ended. "What are we hiding from?"

The edges of Jess's eyes crinkled in mirth.

"I—" Marion stared at Jess as she tried to start thinking again. She blinked. What had she been doing? Why wasn't it kissing Jess? Marion swayed forward as if to kiss her again.

A car door closed loudly behind her followed by laughter drifting toward them through the summer air. Marion shook her head. Right.

"We need to leave," Marion said. She lifted her head and looked around again. Not only did they need to leave, they needed to do it without catching Tabitha's attention.

Jess's arms snaked around Marion's waist. "Are you sure we can't stay just a bit longer?" She nuzzled against Marion's shoulder blade, trailing kisses across the exposed skin there. "We don't even have to move from this spot." She splayed a hand out over Marion's stomach.

Marion swallowed hard against the temptation, but the longer they stayed, the more likely Tabitha was to catch them. She covered Jess's hand with her own and laced their fingers together.

"There's my car." She and Tabitha had arrived together, but Marion knew that Tabitha wouldn't be taking her home at the end of the night. She never did. Marion was always left to fend for herself when Tabitha went home with whichever man caught her attention. This time, Marion wouldn't be going home alone either.

"All right." Jess shook her head in bemusement as she allowed Marion to tug her toward the car. Marion slid into it while Jess gave her address to the driver. She had enough cash to buy his silence when they got to Jess's apartment. That, and the knowledge that he would never work again if he let someone's secrets slip, would keep him from telling anyone about her clandestine escape with Jess.

It was all Marion could do to wait until the car door was closed before she tilted Jess's chin up and caught her lips in a kiss. Jess's lips were warm against hers as she nipped at them. Their lips melded together as the kiss deepened, and Marion felt Jess shiver under her ministrations. She couldn't help but smile.

Marion pulled away long enough to whisper, "You're beautiful," before Jess pressed their lips together once again. Jess's hands found their way into Marion's hair and Marion nearly purred at the light tugging. She wouldn't have noticed the car coming to a stop if it weren't for Jess pulling away.

"Do you still want to come in?" Jess asked. Marion couldn't believe Jess would think she would say no.

"Yes," Marion replied, eager to get out of the car and inside.

"Good," Jess said, then she repeated herself in a whisper, "good." After what felt like an eternity, they finally got out of the car and headed up Jess's front walk. She pulled out her keys and let them in. Marion didn't bother looking around the apartment. She pulled the only thing worth looking at into her arms.

"We're skipping the wine, yes?" Jess asked as she looped her arms around Marion's neck.

"We can have the wine later," Marion replied. She was already looking forward to a long night. Jess grabbed her hand and led her back to the bedroom.

"Do you often seduce wayward musicians at Hollywood parties?" Jess asked. "That is what happened here, isn't it?" Still teasing then. Would Jess be like that in bed? All light touches and quick wit?

"I thought you were the one doing the seducing. We are in your house, after all."

"At your insistence," Jess said as they finally reached her bedroom. Marion watched as Jess unfastened the tie at the top of her halter top. Even though Jess was facing away from her, Marion's mouth went dry. The top panels of fabric fell away leaving Jess bare-breasted. Jess turned around and grabbed Marion's hands to pull them around her waist. "Take this the rest of the way off," Jess said, looking at Marion coyly, and who was Marion to deny her? As soon as she finished with the top, Marion moved on to Jess's skirt. It slid off a moment later. Marion moved her hands over Jess's hips and pulled her close as she leaned in for another kiss.

"You're even more beautiful like this," Marion whispered.

"You've already gotten me into bed, there's no need for flattery," Jess said as she found the zipper to Marion's dress. Marion felt the teeth separating against her skin as Jess pulled it down.

"By my estimation, we are at least three feet from the bed."

"Well, that's much too far away." Jess stepped forward and forced Marion to step back. Soon, Marion had no choice but to climb onto the bed. She sank down into it as Jess climbed on top of her. As Jess straddled her hips, her hands came to Marion's breasts and squeezed them. It made Marion's breath catch in her throat.

"This is better," Marion replied hoarsely.

"I'm glad you think so." Jess stretched forward over Marion's body, pushing Marion's arms up over her head, and brought their lips back together. "Let's see what else I can do to make this night better." Their breasts brushed together, and Marion shuddered.

"You give it your best effort, and I'll give it mine," Marion said before she shifted and rolled them over.

Jess laughed. "Whatever you want, darling."

❖

Marion looked down at Jess, sprawled on her stomach next to her in the bed. Jess's glass of wine sat precariously on the mattress, kept upright by a pair of barely-there fingers. Marion sat up next to her, bare to the waist.

"Is this where you tell me you don't do this sort of thing?" Jess asked as she looked up at Marion. She splayed the fingers of her other hand across Marion's thigh.

"Very rarely do I do this sort of thing." Marion trailed her fingers over the owl tattooed on Jess's shoulder. The bird's wings were unfurling and when Jess shifted it almost looked like the owl was in flight. It was only one of many tattoos that covered Jess's skin, and Marion wanted to explore them all, to hear the stories behind them.

"No, you don't seem the type." Jess smirked. She rolled onto her side and took a sip of her wine. Moonlight spilled in through the open curtains. Marion reached out and cupped Jess's face, brushing over her lips with her thumb. Jess opened her mouth and took Marion's thumb between her teeth, sucking on it lightly. Marion shuddered.

"Do they mean anything?" Marion asked, tilting her face to the side as she continued to look down at Jess's tattoos.

"Most of them, but they aren't particularly profound. The owl is just because I'm a night owl. The constellation, Cancer, doesn't have anything to do with the zodiac." Jess made a face. "I studied one of the stars in it while I was in grad school. They're all things like that. Nothing particularly philosophical."

"You went to grad school?"

"Mm-hmm." Jess took another sip of her wine. "Astrophysics, but the singing thing really started to take off before I could finish." Marion laughed in disbelief.

"Well, my compliments to whoever your artist is. They're all beautiful." Beautiful seemed to be a word she used a lot around Jess. She trailed her hand down Jess's neck to her arm and then down to her hand where she took the glass of wine and set it aside. Then she leaned down and captured Jess's lips in a rosé-scented kiss, bringing her own hand to Jess's side and guiding her onto her back. Jess went willingly.

"I'll pass it along," Jess said after the kiss ended. She reached up and threaded her fingers into Marion's hair, keeping her in place. "But for now, why don't we find another way to spend our time." Jess kissed Marion this time, quickly deepening it. Marion shifted until she was lying next to Jess, their kiss coming to an end. "Because right now, I really want to go down on you."

Marion moaned and canted her hips toward Jess bringing their bodies even closer together. "I'm not stopping you," Marion said.

"Mmm," Jess replied as she pushed Marion onto her back. "Good."

❖

Marion groaned as a slash of light moved back and forth across her eyes. Each pass made her head throb, and when she tried to move her arm to cover her face, she found it wrapped in sheets that distinctly didn't feel like her own. She extracted her limb from its trap, covered her face with her forearm, and slowly opened her eyes.

That was the last time she drank that much scotch followed by that much wine. Now she'd have to pay for it. She stretched into the well-earned soreness of her muscles and looked over to where she assumed Jess would be.

Jess wasn't there.

Then she noticed the sound of the shower. Panic gripped her heart as it started to beat double-time. God, what had she been thinking? What had convinced her to go home with Jess Carmichael of all people? She'd be lucky to get out of there without the paparazzi noticing. She didn't need some sort of lesbian scandal marring a career just gaining traction. Tabitha would murder her. Tabitha only cared about one thing: Marion's career. What Marion's career could do for Tabitha. If something happened to that, if something disrupted Tabitha's plans, Marion didn't want to know how Tabitha would react. It wouldn't be good. If Tabitha was going down, she would drag Marion down with her. And if Marion's night with Jess became public knowledge, it would be all anyone talked about for weeks. There was a serious possibility that she would never work again. She couldn't even blame the scotch; she had made up her mind before she'd even had half of her second glass, at the snarky comment about her Oscar.

Marion slipped out of bed and found her dress. She needed to leave. She needed to leave now. She pulled the dress on as quickly as she could. The shower kept running. It was still running when Marion left the bedroom. It was easy to find her way out of the apartment.

Marion walked several blocks away before she flagged down a taxi. It didn't matter how much she enjoyed Jess's company; she needed to forget that last night had ever happened. She had simply gotten carried away. It wouldn't happen again.

Chapter Three

Present Day

Marion pushed open the door to the studio and walked in. Where other actors might bring an entourage, she preferred to come alone. She had an assistant, but Barbara was too no-nonsense to spend her days babysitting Marion. It was an attitude Marion appreciated. Despite this, she had been tempted to bring Barbara along with her that day. A friendly face in the room would have been worth something, but Marion couldn't bring herself to ask. It would be such an unusual request, it would invite questions Marion wasn't prepared to answer, and so, she was alone. She was, after all, the only one responsible for her performance, and the only one responsible for what she had done to Jess twenty-four years ago. The number of people surrounding her wouldn't change that.

It was time for their read-through as a cast, presumably the only time they would all be together in the same room. For an animated film where they would all be recording their dialogue separately, it was unusual that they were even doing that, but Richard was known for being a bit eccentric, and if he wanted to put them all in the same room, who was she to contradict him? Still, trepidation built in her stomach as she stepped up to the receptionist's desk. A quick exchange later and she had directions back to the conference room where they would be doing the read-through. She wiped oddly damp palms against her trousers before opening the door.

She needn't have worried. The room was empty. Before she could sit, a production assistant came by and asked her if she needed anything. She said no to the coffee and yes to a bottle of water as she settled into the room. A series of tables were set up in a ring large enough to provide seats for each of the cast members, but there was no indication of where she should sit. She took the seat farthest from the entrance: the better to watch the door. She opened her script and started looking through it. She already had her lines memorized but there was no harm in reviewing them again.

Marion easily fell into the character and startled when the door opened a crack. She saw a flash of pink and just had time to process it before the door opened the rest of the way and suddenly Jess stood in front of her. She looked the same. Older, obviously, but otherwise unchanged.

Marion sat up straighter as they made eye contact.

"Marion." Jess spoke before Marion could shake herself from her daze. She didn't know what to say.

"Jessica." It had to be her imagination that Jess flinched when Marion said her name. Their eyes held for what felt like forever but couldn't have been more than a moment. Marion couldn't tell what Jess was thinking. She hadn't been privy to Jess's thoughts in years. The silence stretched into awkwardness. She resisted the urge to shift in her seat.

Jess stepped fully into the room and let the door close behind herself. The click of the latch in the otherwise silent room brought Marion back to herself. How were they supposed to do this? What level of small talk was appropriate? The past hung in the air between them.

"I should have known you would be here early," Jess said.

"Yes, well." Marion shrugged. "Old habits."

"Of course." Jess pulled out a seat by the door, one as far from Marion as possible. After everything, Marion knew she had earned that wariness. Still, she ached at the distance between them.

The awkwardness continued as Jess pulled out her own copy of the script, several pens, and a small notebook from her oversized purse. Marion looked down at her own hands, so much older now than when she first met Jessica Carmichael.

Before she could get too caught up in the past, the door swung open again. A young teenager bounded into the room, with a harried looking woman, presumably her mother, trailing behind.

The girl came to a stop when she noticed the other people in the room. She whispered, "Whoa," under her breath before collecting herself. Jess broke out into a wide smile.

"Hello," Jess greeted her.

"Um, hi." The girl blinked and looked between the two of them. She must be the lead. "I'm Naomi." She wasn't shy. Marion would give her that. Perhaps just a tad overawed, probably more at Jess than at her. Jess had that effect on people. She always had.

"And I'm Judy." The girl's mother puffed. "Now, let's sit down while we wait for everyone else to arrive." She gestured to the room with overburdened arms.

"Okay." Naomi shrugged blithely and took a seat somewhere between Marion and Jess. Judy put down her collection of things on the table and took the seat next to Naomi. Naomi looked between them, not sure who to address first.

"I'm Jess," Jess interjected. "And that's Marion." She pointed across the space between them without so much as glancing at her, and it was friendlier than Marion had any right to expect.

"It's nice to meet you, Je—" Naomi caught a look from her mother. "Ms. Carmichael. Ms. Hargreaves." Of course, Naomi already knew who they were. Marion didn't like to think about her fame, but some things were inevitable. Being recognized most everywhere, particularly someplace where it would behoove people to know exactly who she was, was one of them.

Marion tried to smile, though she knew it came out more as a grimace. Then again, she didn't have a reputation on set as being overly friendly, so there was no need to fake a joviality she didn't feel, not when her stomach was still churning from being in the same room as Jess again. People expected Jess to be warm and open. No one expected her to be anything other than serious, a reputation she didn't have to work to maintain.

The door opened again, and other members of the cast started to filter in. Gwen walked behind Marion's chair and squeezed her shoulder.

"Everything all right, my girl?" Gwen asked as she looked down at Marion.

"Perfectly." Marion found a moment of calm looking at Gwen. Gwen looked at her with such acceptance that Marion felt herself relaxing fractionally.

"Did you know," Gwen looked at Jess, "Marion was barely in her teens, the first time we met. Such an awkward little thing—we had one of the worst chemistry reads I've ever done, but I could just tell she would be extraordinary. As soon as she was out of the room, I insisted the director cast her."

Marion tensed up at the story, at the way Jess's lips pulled back in an uncomfortable version of a smile, at the way Naomi seemed to be hanging off of Gwen's every word. Obliviously, Gwen squeezed her shoulders again.

"You'll have to let me take you to dinner after we've finished here. As a thank you for doing this."

"If you insist." Marion took a breath. She really did enjoy Gwen's company and dinner would be a good time to catch up.

"I do. And I'm so thrilled you've decided to sign on as a producer as well." Jess's eyes flicked over at her as that bit of news became public, but she quickly looked away again. With one last squeeze, Gwen finally moved on and found a seat of her own.

The door to the room opened once again and another blond head peeked around it, as if the woman was assuring herself she was in the right place before she walked in. Marion frowned, blinking. Was that the girl from the Oscars after party? The door swung the rest of the way open. It was. She stepped into the cacophony, looking around furtively. Marion wondered if she even remembered that night. Their eyes caught and the girl turned pink. Apparently, she did. It had really been too much to hope that she'd never see the girl again. Well, she probably wouldn't see her again after the read-through. The girl, Marion really needed to find out her name, sat near Jess and pulled out her script, avoiding Marion's gaze.

As the room began to fill with child actors, the noise grew. In all the commotion, the chattering of hyperactive children, the loud conversations between parents who had obviously seen each other at auditions before, and Gwen and Richard having a slightly deaf conversation about the script, Marion could finally distract herself from Jess. She looked down at her script, reviewed her notes, and waited for Richard to start the meeting.

After a few minutes, he clapped his hands to get everyone's attention.

"Thank you all for being here. Not that I gave you much choice," he said. Polite laughter filled the room. "Don't worry, I won't force you all into some sort of acting game. I'd rather jump straight in. I'm sure we can all learn each other's names as we go. I do want to introduce Gwen Harrington and Marion Hargreaves as they're both executive producers on this project. We're going to do our best not to piss them off, right?" There was more polite laughter, though the undercurrent of discomfort felt stronger. Marion could have done without Richard bringing it up.

Jess was looking at her again, as if she couldn't work something out, vague worry pulling at her lips. Marion met her eyes and Jess turned her attention back to Richard.

"Now, Naomi, you're where we start. Let's go."

Almost as soon as the read-through ended, Jess practically jumped to her feet, made an excuse about her driver, and fled the room. Well, at least they wouldn't have to make more pained small talk. Marion gathered her things more slowly giving Jess time to get out of the building before she followed. Gwen squeezed her shoulder again as she passed behind her.

"Finnegan's at eight?" she asked. Marion nodded. She remembered that the venerable old restaurant was one of Gwen's favorites. She probably had a table waiting for her already.

She took one last look around the room. Some of the parents were still stuffing things into the ubiquitous bags that seemed to accompany children everywhere no matter how old they were. She stood and gathered her things. She was ready to leave when she heard someone clear their throat behind her.

"Ms. Hargreaves?" Marion turned. It was the young woman from the Oscars party. Lauren something. She remembered the film she had been in now. Mobsters. Prestigious director. She'd enjoyed the performance if not the violence. It had felt rather try-hard in its provocation.

"Yes?" God, she hoped the girl wasn't about to try to come on to her again. She put on her most imperious look.

"I just wanted to apologize about the other night." Lauren wrapped a hand around the strap of her purse and tugged on it. "I was, well, pretty far gone, or I never would have said those things. Um, thank you for getting me to my car. I promise, I don't normally drink that much. The champagne just sort of snuck up on me."

Marion fractionally relaxed her shoulders. If she was apologizing, there was no need to run the girl off. "Apology accepted. And though I don't expect we'll see much of one another, I suppose you should call me Marion."

"Uh, sure. I'm Lauren. I guess we never really got introduced." Lauren rocked back and forth on her feet.

"I'll endeavor to remember that. For the next time I have to pour you into a car." A smile tugged at Marion's lips.

Lauren blushed again. "Yeah. Thanks. Thank you."

"Was there anything else?"

"No." Lauren shook her head as she rushed to reassure her. "I should let you go. I really just wanted to explain, not take up your time. You should…yeah. It was good talking to you."

"You as well." Marion nodded, turned toward the door, and left.

❖

Low light filtered through the restaurant's dining room as Marion settled into her seat and finally let some of the tension from the day bleed away. Gwen should be there any minute and they could have a pleasant meal and catch up. They hadn't really spoken in a couple of years, but constant contact didn't define their relationship. Marion looked around and saw the maître d' leading Gwen across the room.

She smiled up at Gwen as she allowed the maître d' to pull out her chair and help her into it. After pulling her chair in, Gwen looked at Marion.

"All right, out with it." Gwen pulled her napkin onto her lap then looked up at Marion with piercing eyes. Marion startled.

"Out with what?" she asked, confused as to what Gwen might be referencing.

"Whatever's going on with you." Gwen folded her hands together. "You were phoning it in the entire afternoon, and you have too much integrity to do that unless something is wrong. So. What's wrong?"

Marion met Gwen's eyes and thought about denying it. Gwen raised an eyebrow, daring her to try.

"Jess Carmichael and I—we've met before. It didn't go well." She hoped that would be enough for Gwen. She really didn't feel like getting into the details, particularly somewhere where they might be overheard.

"Ah." Gwen looked at her with knowing eyes. Maybe Marion wouldn't need to tell Gwen all about it after all. "The past can be distracting at times." She nodded in understanding.

"But you know, you really shouldn't judge someone just because she wears bright colors and sings pop songs." Gwen lifted her wine glass and took a sip as Marion frowned. She had hoped Gwen wouldn't think her that shallow.

"That isn't—" Marion sighed and deflated before taking her own wine glass. She couldn't tell Gwen what had happened. She wouldn't understand. "You're right." She took a sip. "I'll just have to try to be more open-minded."

Gwen brightened. "Good." She nodded as if that settled the matter. "I've had this brilliant idea and I've already talked to the rest of the cast, at least the adult members of the cast. We're all going out for drinks together a few nights from now. You simply have to come. I won't let you say no."

Marion sighed. "Well, if I can't say no, I suppose I'll be there." It wasn't her favorite way to pass a night, but at least there would only be a few people involved.

"Excellent. Now, tell me what's been going on with you. It's been forever since I've seen you."

❖

1997

Marion walked into one of the lesser-known establishments in West Hollywood, not certain what to expect. It could be anything from a vegan restaurant to a tattoo parlor, but it looked like a perfectly sedate café. Julia Melendez, one of the top ranked tennis players in the world, was hosting a small group of friends and hadn't let Marion beg off, as she was inclined to do. She and Julia had met the year before when Marion had attended one of the many tournaments Julia had handily won. They'd quickly become friends, bonding over having such high expectations placed on them at such young ages. And with Julia came a whole set of Julia's friends. The group never seemed to have exactly the same people in it twice, but they were always engaging and entertaining and just the sort of young Hollywood glitterati that Tabitha approved of. Still, the party the night before, the encounter with Jess, had left her exhausted. Staying up all night didn't suit her. She was mildly sore and mildly hungover and being at home with a cup of tea sounded better than having to socialize, but there she was anyway.

She caught sight of Julia on the other side of the restaurant and started to make her way over to the group. Looking them over, she found she knew most of them, a particularly eclectic group, but she knew most of the members and enjoyed their company. Marion's steps stuttered as she saw familiar blond hair. Jess? What were the odds? Apparently, odds didn't matter because there she was. Marion wondered if she could slip out after all.

"Marion!" Julia lit up when she saw Marion. She held her hand out. Marion no longer had a choice. She wouldn't be getting out of this dinner now that Julia had seen her. Julia was always dragging her into things like this.

"Julia." Marion crossed the rest of the distance between them. Julia reached for her and Marion awkwardly returned the one-armed hug and kiss on the cheek.

As Marion drew back, Julia turned to her side. "I know you know everybody else, but have you met Jess Carmichael?"

Images of Jess spread out beneath her flashed into Marion's mind. How should she answer? "Briefly." Marion looked at Jess and offered her hand. Jess bit back a smirk as they shook hands and exchanged pleasantries. Marion supposed *brief meeting* defined their relationship well enough thus far. They hadn't exactly spent much time getting to know one another outside of bed. They certainly weren't friends.

Marion raised an eyebrow as Jess pushed out the seat next to her in invitation, smiling impishly. Marion didn't have much choice but to take it and she wondered how Jess knew Julia. Julia didn't often travel in the same circles as actors and musicians, but then again, Marion and Jess didn't exactly travel in the same circles either, and they had run into each other twice in as many days.

Marion barely paid attention to the rest of the reintroductions, too aware of Jess sitting next to her to focus.

"So, what's the occasion?" Jess asked as she set her menu aside. She'd barely glanced at it. Maybe she came to the café on a regular basis. Marion had no way of knowing.

"No occasion." Julia shrugged. "Season's about to start, and then I won't have the time or energy for you people. So, I thought I'd get a last bit of socializing in before Coach has me running sprints at dawn." She laughed, clearly eager to get started despite her words.

The rest of the table joined in the laughter. Marion went to sip at her wine but flinched and nearly choked when Jess's hand found her thigh. At least the laughter probably covered it. She looked down at the hand then over at Jess in question. What did Jess think she was doing? Still, Marion did nothing to dissuade her or the fingertips that were now tracing shapes against the exposed skin just above her knee.

The conversation meandered from tennis, to some of the group's latest projects, to Bill Clinton and politics, but Marion could only just keep up. Jess's hand kept distracting her. Jess's nails scratched over her skin, raising goose bumps and making her shiver. She swallowed hard and shifted in her seat. A look over to Jess got a knowing look in return. Jess knew exactly what she was doing. Marion didn't know if she wanted Jess to stop or keep going.

The hand slipped toward the inside of her thigh and up higher. She clutched at the edge of the table.

Jess laughed at something and it startled Marion, drawing her attention back to the table. No one was paying attention to her or had noticed her lapse into introspection.

"Everything all right, Marion?" Julia asked. Apparently, Julia had noticed after all.

"I'm fine." Marion removed the napkin from her lap. "If you'll excuse me for a moment." She stood from the table and headed toward the restroom, her stomach full of butterflies.

She pushed into the small room, just two stalls and two sinks, and exhaled heavily. She turned on the tap and thrust her wrists under the water. She didn't know how long she stood there trying to catch her breath and cool off. She didn't know how she could stand finishing the meal if Jess kept teasing her.

Her insides were twisted in knots. She wanted her heart to stop beating so fast, she wanted to wipe that smug look off of Jess Carmichael's face, but more than anything she wanted to drag Jess back to her apartment and spend the rest of the day in bed with her. She felt the ghost of Jess's fingers on her thigh.

She grabbed a paper towel and wiped her hands dry. She had just tossed it away when the door opened again. Marion looked up. Jess. She should have known. Their eyes met in the mirror and held. As they stared at each other, the speed of Marion's heartbeat doubled. The air grew thick and Marion could barely breathe. Tension stretched out between them waiting for the slightest movement to break it.

Jess sucked in a loud breath. At least, it seemed loud in the too-quiet bathroom. "Are you—" Her voice trembled.

The tension snapped. Marion spun around and surged across the space between them. She crashed their lips together, her tongue already swiping across Jess's lower lip, asking for entry. Jess opened her mouth at the touch.

What was she doing? How did Jess drive her so crazy? She could still feel Jess's fingers on the inside of her knee. She could still feel Jess's fingers inside her. She wanted that again. Jess had her aching for it.

Jess met Marion with equal fervor, tongues sliding together as hands grasped and groped at each other. Marion pulled Jess closer, wedged her thigh between Jess's, and pushed her up against the counter.

Jess, Jess, Jess.

She wrenched her lips away only to start kissing her way down Jess's neck. Jess's fingers tangled in Marion's hair as she bucked against Marion's thigh.

"We're not going to have sex in the ladies', are we?" Marion gasped against Jess's neck. She reached down to grab Jess's ass.

"We are if you don't stop doing that," Jess replied, grinding down on Marion's thigh. She bit down on Marion's shoulder through her shirt and Marion sucked in a breath at the dull pain.

"I don't want to stop." Marion started rucking up Jess's skirt. She couldn't believe they were about to do this, that she was about to do this. Jess sent her out of her head. She had never done anything so reckless in her life. If someone walked in on them, or if anyone found out, Tabitha would do everything she could to destroy her because of the scandal it would create. But that thought didn't stop her.

"Then I guess we're having sex here after all." Jess wriggled to help Marion with her skirt. As soon as it was up far enough, Marion swept Jess's underwear to the side and dipped her fingers into Jess's wetness. Jess bit back a moan and tilted her hips forward. "But after this, you're taking me home where we can do this properly."

"Whatever you want." Marion rubbed her fingers over Jess's clit. She didn't do it with much finesse, but she didn't need to. She remembered just enough of what Jess liked from the night before to be able to hit the right points to leave Jess gasping and clutching at her as she threw a leg over Marion's hip to pull her closer. Marion pushed a finger inside of Jess and gasped at the tight warmth.

Jess's hips jolted forward, and with another sweep of Marion's thumb, she fell apart in Marion's arms. Marion held Jess as she calmed, kissing the corner of her mouth until Jess turned her head and met Marion's lips with her own. They kissed slowly, deeply as Marion pulled Jess's skirt back down.

Eventually, they had to disentangle themselves. "How soon do you think we can get out of here?" Jess nuzzled against Marion's cheek.

"I don't see any reason to stay for dessert, do you?" Marion let Jess go and turned to the sink to wash her hands. Once again, the cool water did little to slow her racing heart. She ached for Jess to touch her, but despite what they had just done, it wasn't the time or place.

After she dried her hands, she ran her fingers through her hair, setting it to rights again. She listened as Jess took a deep breath and started to do the same. She had just finished when Jess knocked their shoulders together and started giggling.

"No," Jess said while still laughing, "I don't think I'll be sampling anything on the *restaurant's* dessert menu." Marion blushed. They could have sex in the restroom and she was fine, but the slightest bit of innuendo had her cheeks on fire. It only made Jess laugh more. She leaned in and kissed Marion's cheek. "Go back to the table. I'll join you in a few minutes and we can make our excuses."

Marion nodded, took a moment to further compose herself, then headed back out. She would come up with an excuse for Julia as to why she and Jess needed to leave together later.

❖

It was early evening and Marion stared at her phone, the cord curled over her knee. Her apartment felt vast and empty, a place designed to look appropriate for intimate magazine interviews and not to live in. Nothing in it felt comfortable.

It had been a week and a half since she had last seen Jess, after they had stumbled back to Jess's apartment at the end of Julia's party, and her skin itched to feel Jess's hands again. Was she allowed? Tabitha would certainly say that she wasn't, but Tabitha was in New York on business and not there to look over Marion's shoulder. Could she really do it? Both of her prior encounters with Jess had happened by chance. This would be deliberate.

Marion swallowed down her nervousness and picked up the handset. She dialed the number before she could change her mind and held her breath as the phone rang.

"Hello, this is Jess." The sound of Jess's voice caught Marion off guard and she couldn't say anything. Silence stretched out. "Hello?"

Marion shook herself out of her thoughts. "Jess, it's Marion." After that, she floundered.

"Oh, hi." Marion could hear Jess's smile. "You know, when I gave you my number, I didn't think you'd ever actually use it."

Marion blushed. "I hadn't planned on it, but…" She tangled her fingers in the phone cord.

"But I'm irresistible." Jess laughed and Marion supposed that Jess was right. Somehow, she couldn't resist Jess even though she desperately needed to.

"If that's how you want to see yourself." Marion tried for blasé, but she wasn't sure she pulled it off.

"I do. That's exactly how I want to see myself. Besides, you're the one who called me. You've only proven my point."

Jess had her there. "Well, you're certainly something." It was all Marion would admit to.

"As much as I'm enjoying this conversation, I would much rather enjoy it in person," Jess said, and Marion's breath caught again. That's what she had wanted, right? That was why she had called Jess in the first place.

"I…" Why was this so hard? Marion twisted her fingers even more tightly into the cord.

"Just tell me how long it's going to take you to get here." Jess's voice turned husky and it made Marion flush.

"Half an hour." She was barely able to say it, but once it was out, there was no taking it back. She pulled her fingers free and started looking for her shoes.

Chapter Four

Present Day

Marion sat placidly in the waiting room outside of Richard's office, back straight, knees lined up with toes and hands on her lap, hoping that the director would make an appearance soon. The office didn't fit what she knew of the man, full of dark wood and heavy furniture, but the bright, vintage animation cels which lined the walls provided a counterpoint to the seriousness. Marion didn't know why Richard wanted to see her, only that he had requested her presence before she was set to record her scenes later in the week. The sound of footsteps reverberated from the adjoining hallway and Marion refocused on the room as the door opened.

Marion's feeling of calm from that morning disappeared, and she tensed with nerves as Jess walked into the room.

"Oh, Marion." Jess stopped short, ponytail swinging behind her. There were only a few chairs in the outer office and rather than sit, Jess crossed her arms and stepped to the side of the room.

"Jessica." Marion nodded and there was that flinch again, just the slightest recoiling as Marion said her name.

It seemed she had hurt Jess as badly as she had suspected if even saying her name caused Jess to recoil. Marion wouldn't force any other interaction on her. Acknowledging each other was polite, they could do that much. Recording the dialogue for the film wouldn't have them interacting, and Jess could always push off the recording sessions for Marion's songs onto an assistant.

Jess rocked onto the balls of her feet then back to her heels as she stared at the ground. It gave Marion the opportunity to really look at Jess for the first time since the read-through.

She had been right. Jess looked older now. Older, but no less captivating. From this distance, Marion could see the slight crow's feet at the corners of Jess's eyes, the laugh lines around her mouth, but otherwise her skin was smooth, just as it had always been. New tattoos graced her arms, though she couldn't make out what they were. Even in this quiet, tense moment, she shone with some sort of ineffable charisma that had Marion wanting to smile. She pursed her lips against it.

Jess kept subtly rocking back and forth, nerves of some sort taking hold of her.

"Do you…" Jess briefly looked at Marion with worry in her eyes before she looked away again. Still, Marion knew what she was trying to ask.

"Do I know why we're here?" Marion met Jess's eyes as she looked up again, confirming Marion's suspicion. "No. I don't."

Jess nodded but kept her arms crossed over her stomach. Quiet fell back over the room. Jess pulled out her phone and did something on it, texting perhaps. It only took her a few seconds though before she slid it back into her purse.

"I just…does it always feel like you've been pulled into the principal's office?" Jess shrugged.

"I wouldn't know." Marion swallowed uncomfortably and looked away. Her parents had started her acting early, and as such, she'd had private tutors until she had escaped for a brief stint at university.

"Right." Jess nodded.

"If it helps, I doubt it's unpleasant. As we haven't started yet, he can't have any reason to be unhappy with us." Marion finally met Jess's eyes. She wanted to assuage Jess's worries, to calm her, but beyond those words, she couldn't. Jess wouldn't want Marion to touch her, to rub her back or hold her hands. Marion had done everything possible to make sure of that.

Jess nodded again, smile still tight. "Thank you."

Before they could lapse back into uncomfortable silence, Richard shuffled into the outer office. "Oh good, you're both here." He motioned for them to follow him into his personal office, holding the door as Jess, then Marion, entered the room. This office was more what Marion expected, messy and colorful, and she thought she saw building blocks on one of the side tables.

"I'll keep this brief," Richard said as he leaned against his desk. "I want you two to record your scenes together." He clapped his hands and looked expectantly between them.

Jess opened her mouth to say something, but nothing came out. Marion tried to master her own incredulity. This wasn't happening.

"I really think it will give us the emotion that I want. Really make the audience feel the tension between the characters before they reconcile." Richard pumped his fist. "I want to make the audience really feel it when they make peace. It's such a major character beat for Hestia. It'll get the audience behind her. Create some sympathy for an otherwise hard-nosed character."

"Of course." Marion gave a clipped nod. It seemed she and Jess would be spending at least an afternoon together as they recorded.

"You're the director," Jess said, smile tight.

"Excellent!" Richard reached out and clapped both of them on their shoulders. Jess moved with the force while Marion did her best to look unaffected. "My assistant will come up with a time that works for all of us and we'll be good to go." He rubbed his hands together. "Now, you can both go back to your days." His eyes twinkled as he sent them away.

Marion waited for Jess to precede her out of Richard's office, then closed the door behind them, but Jess stopped short before they could leave the outer office. She turned around and wrung her hands together. She opened her mouth, closed it, then opened it again.

"I can't pretend to understand why you did it." Jess shook her head, eyes focused somewhere over Marion's shoulder. "I thought...well, it doesn't really matter what I thought, does it?" She looked at Marion searchingly.

"Jess—" Marion started only to be cut off when Jess held up a hand.

"I think...that is..." Jess's throat worked. "Since we have to work together, let's just forget about it. It was a long time ago."

Marion nodded. "If that's what you want." Jess's suggestion was for the best. They would just act like nothing had ever happened between them and everything would be fine.

"It is." Jess looked away then back at Marion again before turning and walking away.

"Marion." She hadn't heard Richard's door open, but she turned after he called her name.

"Yes?"

"I wanted to ask a favor." Richard put his hands in his pockets. "I was hoping you'd take her under your wing a bit. She's never acted before. Maybe take her to coffee, give her some pointers."

"You mean Jess?" Marion pointed toward the door Jess had just left through.

"Yes, quite." Richard smiled and it made his eyes twinkle. "Why don't you let me set something up? I'm sure if you spend some time together, you'll get on famously."

Marion pursed her lips.

"I suppose that's fine," she agreed but only because all of her free time was booked for the next few days. There was no way she and Jess would have time to get together before they recorded their scenes, and meeting after that would be pointless.

"Excellent." Richard nodded emphatically. "And thank you." He opened the door to his office and held it open for Marion.

"It's no bother," Marion said before she turned and left.

"Richard's assistant called while you were out." Barbara shuffled through Marion's mail, sorting it into piles as part of some system Marion didn't even try to decipher, while Marion flipped through a script Margaret had sent over.

Marion sat on a barstool in her kitchen as Barbara managed the minutia of Marion's life.

Marion looked up from her script. "And?"

"And you have coffee with Jess tomorrow at two. You start recording the day after."

"Coffee?" Marion said with a strangled voice as her grip on her script tightened. She had thought coffee would be impossible. Her schedule was full, and there was no way Jess would agree to have coffee with her. She thought she would have at least a few days to get used to the idea of spending time with Jess again. A few days to steel herself for the inevitable stress of being in the same room with someone who had set the course for so much of Marion's life, even if Jess didn't know it.

Barbara started opening the mail, letter opener slicing through the paper envelopes, unaware of the turmoil her words had inspired.

"McAllister canceled, so you happened to have a free afternoon tomorrow. It was nothing to replace him with Jess."

"You—" Marion shook her head. She couldn't believe this was happening. How was she supposed to sit across from Jess and give her acting tips? Why had Jess even said yes to the meeting?

"Do you want me to call you a car or will you drive yourself?"

Marion barely heard the question. All she could think about was surviving coffee with Jess. And assuming she did survive, in two days' time she would be trapped in a recording booth with Jess and her tattoos and her perfume. Her head spun. She put a hand to her temple. There had to be a way for her to get out of it all. Did she still have time to drop out of the movie? No. She couldn't do that. She had made a commitment.

At Marion's lack of response, Barbara finally looked up from the mail.

"Did you hear me?" Barbara pursed her lips.

Marion shook her head. "What was that?" She couldn't for the life of her recall what Barbara had just asked her.

"I asked if you wanted—you know what, never mind." Barbara pulled down a wine glass and grabbed the open bottle from the counter. She pulled the cork out and poured a glass then slid it in front of Marion. Marion looked up at her questioningly.

"I didn't—" Marion shook her head. She rarely drank during the day. She wasn't sure why Barbara was encouraging it now.

"No, you didn't. But you sure as hell look like you need it." Barbara pushed the glass a little closer and Marion had to pick it up or risk it falling off of the island. She automatically took a sip.

"Thank you." Marion looked down at the glass in her hand.

"What's your beef with the queen of the Top 40?" Barbara asked. "I've never seen someone knock you for a loop like this."

"There is no, that is, I don't…" Marion shook her head, tried to shake off the way even just hearing Jess's name affected her. Barbara raised both of her eyebrows. Marion deflated. "We have a past." She took a deep breath. "But it was more than twenty years ago."

"Twenty years is a long time." Barbara looked at Marion sympathetically. Barbara had worked for Marion for so long, there wasn't much she didn't know about her life, but she didn't know about Jess. No one knew about Jess. And that was the point, wasn't it?

"Not long enough, it seems." Marion smiled a tight smile then took a sip of her wine. Seeing Jess again though, it brought up so many old feelings, both good and bad. The attraction, certainly, Jess was still one of the most attractive people Marion had ever met, but also the way everything had crashed and burned in the end, and how all of it had been her fault. If she could go back, she would do it differently. Even if things wouldn't have lasted, she would have found some way to avoid causing Jess so much pain.

1997

Marion lay on Jess's mattress and stared up at the ceiling as the shower ran in the background. This was her cue, familiar and repeated. She needed to get up. She needed to leave. If she didn't leave, she'd want to stay. She'd want to stay for days and days, until Jess got sick of her and kicked her out. This had become a very bad habit and she needed to stop. They would get caught eventually, and then everything would be all over. Her life, her career, Jess's career, everything. Tabitha would see to it. So much of her life had centered around keeping Tabitha happy, being the perfect blank slate for directors to project their character onto just as Tabitha wanted. There was no future in this, but Marion desperately wanted there to be. She wanted to be able to say no to Tabitha, to break free of her hold, but Marion didn't know how. How was she supposed to break away from one of the few touchstones in her life? Maybe

Jess was just a fling, but maybe she wasn't. Maybe they could have something real. Except they couldn't. Of course, they couldn't. Not while Jess was a secret she could never reveal.

Marion was just lifting herself up onto her elbows when the door to the bathroom opened and startled her, pulling her from the moroseness she was quickly falling into.

"You don't need to sneak out, you know." Jess leaned against the doorframe, unbothered by her own nudity. Marion tried not to stare. It was a losing battle. If Jess was around, Marion didn't want to do anything other than look at her.

Marion couldn't really deny it. That was exactly what she had been about to do. It was something she needed to do. Tabitha was already suspicious, already checking in to make sure Marion wasn't doing anything she didn't approve of. Marion felt the fear of it in her chest, squeezing her lungs.

Jess smirked and padded over to the bed, crawling onto it and on top of Marion. Marion sank back down into the bed as Jess straddled her hips, her fear overridden by desire.

"Don't worry so much." Jess leaned down and kissed Marion's lips, lingering over them. "I'm not under any illusions about what this is, but this is also the fourth time we've ended up back in my apartment and in my bed. I think we've progressed to taking a shower together and having a cup of coffee while we wait for your cab to get here, don't you?" Jess kissed her again.

Marion exhaled and felt the tension melt from her body. "I suppose that would be acceptable."

Jess smiled slowly. "Good. Now come get in the shower." She pulled away from Marion and got up, walking toward the bathroom without looking back.

Marion rolled out of the bed and followed after Jess, getting into the shower without stopping to think about what getting home late might mean. Surely Tabitha wouldn't call her on a Saturday morning to make sure she was home.

She ducked her head and kissed the water from Jess's shoulder, wrapping her arms around Jess in the humid shower stall.

"Mmm." Jess twisted around and brought their lips together.

❖

Marion unlocked her front door and walked into her house. The red light was flashing on the answering machine. She didn't have to listen to the message to know who had called. Tabitha. Of course, it would be Tabitha.

She would need to come up with an excuse for why she hadn't been at home when she called. Maybe she could convince Tabitha she had taken up running or something. Anything to explain her absence, even if it was only vaguely plausible.

"Girl." Marion jumped, startled by the voice that seemed to come out of nowhere. Really, Tabitha was standing in her kitchen, out of view of the front door. Marion's eyes went wide. What was she supposed to do now? She hadn't anticipated Tabitha being in her home that morning. She couldn't very well tell Tabitha she had gone running while wearing her clothes from the day before. Luckily, Tabitha hadn't seen her yesterday. It was Marion's saving grace.

"Tabitha. I was just…" Marion shifted nervously. "I was out getting tea." The excuse was plausible enough.

How long ago had Tabitha called? Please, God, let it have been that morning and not the night before.

"I hope it was a very good cup of tea. It certainly took you long enough." Tabitha looked at Marion with narrowed eyes, as if looking hard enough might reveal all of Marion's secrets. Until recently, Marion hadn't had any secrets worth knowing.

"I didn't know you would be here. If I had..." Marion trailed off under Tabitha's withering glare.

"See that it doesn't happen again."

Marion nodded. She would have to be more careful. She couldn't risk Tabitha getting suspicious about her whereabouts. "It won't."

"Good. We have work to do."

Chapter Five

Present Day

Perched on the edge of an overstuffed chair, Marion shivered as the door to the coffee shop opened and cold air blew inside. There was no sense in getting comfortable. She doubted she would be there long. What could she possibly have to say to Jess? After the way they had left everything, there was no coming back from that. That Jess had even agreed to the coffee was baffling, but still, Marion couldn't help but hope, hope that maybe things weren't as bad as she remembered them being. Maybe Jess was willing to at least talk to her. The very thought made Marion's stomach churn with nervousness. She sipped tea from a large mug hoping to calm herself. At least Barbara had scheduled them to meet at Marion's favorite coffee shop, which only nominally served coffee and instead had a wide-ranging tea selection.

Marion glanced at her watch. Two o'clock and Jess was nowhere to be seen. Maybe Jess simply wouldn't show up and they could avoid this farce altogether. Movement in the corner of her eye caught Marion's attention, and she looked out the window at the front of the shop. Jess stood outside taking selfies with a couple of teenage girls. So that's why she was late. Only the bravest of fans ever asked Marion for a photo and for that Marion was thankful.

Jess pulled herself away from her fans and stepped into the coffee shop. Marion knew the moment Jess saw her. The relaxed, easy air she'd had with the teenagers evaporated. Jess didn't bother to come over before she got in line for her coffee. The shop wasn't overly busy, so it only took a few moments for Jess to place her order. Still, each passing moment increased Marion's blood pressure.

With a smile, Jess finally accepted her coffee from a flustered barista and headed toward Marion. She took the seat opposite Marion without saying a word and then wrapped her hands around her mug.

"Richard said we should meet." Jess looked at Marion warily. "He didn't say why though."

"Didn't he?" Marion tapped a finger against the handle of her mug. She drew her shoulders back as she looked over Jess's shoulder and outside. She stared at the people going down the sidewalk as she tried to gather her thoughts.

Jess huffed. "If you aren't going to tell me why I'm here, I'm going to leave." She put her mug down and started to gather her things.

Marion's attention snapped back to Jess. "Don't—" She cleared her throat. God, she should just let Jess go, and tell Richard that they were just too busy to get together before their recording session the next day.

"Don't leave." Marion put her mug down. "I'm sorry. I thought Richard would have said why." She shook her head. "Richard wanted me to give you some acting pointers. This was his idea."

"So, Richard doesn't trust me?" Jess asked. She didn't look any more inclined to stay than she had the moment before.

"I'm certain that isn't it." Even acting on behalf of someone else, it seemed she couldn't find the right thing to say to Jess. "I'm certain he simply thought this would be reassuring."

"I'm not reassured."

"No, I don't suppose you would be." Marion had no clue what sort of actor Jess would turn out to be, but surely, she wouldn't be walking in unprepared. Agreeing to be Richard's go-between had been an idiotic idea. Marion looked down at her hands. "Still, if there's any way I can help." She finally looked back up at Jess, looking for some sort of acceptance of her offer.

"If I wanted a lesson from you, I'd watch your episode of *Inside the Actor's Studio*." Jess rolled her eyes.

Marion pursed her lips. "I was just trying to help."

"Like you *helped* the last time we talked?" Jess's eyes flashed. Marion sucked in a breath. Any illusion she had about getting through this project without discussing the past flew out the window. So did any hope that Jess might have forgiven her, that they might start over.

"I did what was best. I made the only decision I could." Marion tried to keep her voice low. There was no sense in drawing the entire coffee shop into their conversation.

"Fuck you," Jess spat back.

"I did what I had to do. And this isn't the time or place to have this conversation." Marion set her jaw. Didn't Jess understand that they were in public? Anyone could overhear them.

"I'm not interested in hearing your lies anyway." Jess started to gather up her things. "We can record our scenes together and I'll do what I have to, to promote the movie, but that's it. If it isn't about that, don't talk to me again." Jess shook her head as she looked down at Marion. She threw the strap of her purse over her shoulder and walked out.

Marion looked around the coffee shop. Other than a few mildly curious gazes, no one seemed to have paid them any attention. For that, she was thankful. It had been just the disaster she had predicted, but it was over now. She had survived. She finished up her tea, took both her and Jess's mugs to the counter, and left the coffee shop. She tried not to let her anger and disappointment bleed through to the surface. The rest of her day was full, and she had those damn drinks that night, Gwen's plan finally coming to fruition. She needed to get on with it and she didn't have time to deal with all of the feelings that came with interacting with Jess once again.

Marion stepped into the bar and looked around for Gwen and the other adult members of the cast. Gwen had decided they all needed to *bond,* though Marion didn't particularly see the logic. Outside of her upcoming recording session with Jess, she hadn't anticipated spending any time with the rest of the cast. But Gwen had asked, and she hadn't been able to say no, so here she was stepping into Jeffrey's Bar, a surprisingly trendy place given that Gwen had picked it, and one that Marion would normally avoid like the plague. It was still early in the night though, and the music was low enough that she could still hear herself think. She finally spotted Gwen and Richard as they sat huddled together in a corner.

She cautiously approached them, looking for anyone else who might be with them. Jess, she was looking for Jess. Perhaps Jess had managed to say no to Gwen and they wouldn't spend all night tiptoeing around each other. After their coffee earlier in the day, she wasn't sure she was ready to spend a night fending off pointed barbs. Richard and Gwen looked like they were alone though. Maybe she was the only person to take Gwen up on her invitation and she could spend a pleasant night with just the two of them.

"Gwen, Richard." She nodded at both of them as she pulled a barstool up to their table.

"Marion, I'm so glad you could make it." Gwen reached out a hand and Marion took it for a quick squeeze.

"You know I wouldn't be anywhere else tonight." Marion tried to keep the sarcasm out of her voice.

"I know you would absolutely be anywhere else tonight, but you've come anyway, and I thank you for that. I just thought it would be good for us all to get to know each other, smooth out some of the rough edges maybe." Gwen smiled over at Marion, then her eyes flicked to somewhere behind her. "Oh look, Lauren is here, and Jewel and Dave." She waved them over. Still no Jess.

The trio of younger actors, all of whom played teachers in the film, got to the table and joined them, all of them skirting around to the opposite side of the table, as if sitting next to her might incur her wrath. Surely, she wasn't that intimidating.

Before she could say anything about it, a server appeared at her elbow. They gave her their drink orders.

"Jess said she might be a bit late." Gwen looked between them all. "But I don't think we need to wait on her. We can have fun without our resident superstar." Gwen said it teasingly, but Marion flinched nevertheless. "Why don't we all go around and talk about our favorite roles? Get to know each other a bit better. Marion will start."

"I will?" Marion pulled back in surprise. She would? She didn't know what her answer could possibly be, but everyone was looking at her.

"Of course, you will." Gwen looked at her in expectation.

"I haven't thought about my roles in that way. I suppose it's whatever I'm doing next. I prefer not to think about the past." What else could she say? She had certainly enjoyed some films over others, but she hadn't thought about picking a favorite. She heard a sigh from across the table and found Lauren looking at her.

"You don't like my answer?" Marion asked.

Lauren shrugged. "It isn't much of an answer, is it?" She looked at Marion hopefully.

Marion caved and shook her head at herself for doing so. "If I must pick one, Alexandra Gideon in *Night Music.*"

"The junkie?" That was Jewel.

Marion shrugged diffidently. "She was a challenge." She did like a challenge. Not something she particularly expected from *Petunia's Potion*, but this project came with more personal challenges.

"And that scene with the dress is iconic. Was that a body double?" Dave asked.

At that, Marion blushed. She'd forgotten that the part had involved the only nude scene she'd ever agreed to do. She ignored the heat on her cheeks and met Dave's eyes square on.

"It was most certainly not a body double." Marion drew herself up to her full height. As if she would take the easy way out. It was the first part she'd taken after hiring Margaret, and

Margaret had pushed her to consider it, something different. A break from her past. She had needed a break just then, and finding Margaret and her quick friendship had been a balm after she finally managed to move on from Tabitha. She imagined seeing her in the role made Tabitha seethe. She'd be lying if she said that hadn't influenced her decision making. It had felt so freeing to take a part that Tabitha never would have picked for her, too edgy would have been Tabitha's opinion, and too much of a risk for Marion to take the role on. She had loved every minute of it. Even when she had to stand naked in front of the cast and crew.

Something about the way she said it must have been amusing, as the entire table started laughing.

"What are we laughing about?" Marion would have known Jess's voice anywhere, whether she was expecting her or not. For a moment, she had forgotten that Jess would be arriving sometime soon. She sounded much more light-hearted than she had earlier in the day.

"Marion's nude scene," Dave supplied as he looked up at where Jess was standing behind Marion.

"Ah." Jess slid into the only remaining barstool which happened to be next to Marion.

"Didn't you do that *Vogue* shoot naked?" Lauren asked. "I remember tattoos and body paint." Marion remembered that edition of *Vogue*. She remembered it too well.

Jess shrugged. "It was fun." She wasn't looking at Marion though.

"I'm pretty sure that cover was part of my gay awakening." Lauren laughed at herself and Jess joined in.

"I'll take the compliment," Jess said.

"So, Lauren," Marion swiveled toward her, "what's your favorite role?" If it suddenly felt like Lauren was the center of attention, then so be it.

Lauren blushed. "This is going to sound dumb, but I played Sarah Brown in *Guys and Dolls* my freshman year of high school. It was the last thing I did before I got cast in *Jennifer's World*, and if I'm honest, it's the last time I really enjoyed acting." Marion was vaguely aware of *Jennifer's World*, one of those shows for young teenagers on one of those channels that specialized in those sorts of things. It wasn't something she had ever seen or ever wanted to see, but she supposed it did well in its demographics. And Lauren must be able to act, or she wouldn't have been cast in anything since the show had wrapped.

"I don't know. She was just so far away from me. It's what I like most about acting. Getting to be someone completely different from who I am."

Marion nodded. She could respect that, could empathize with it. She felt Jess shifting beside her.

Jewel interjected, "Well, some of us aren't that deep. I liked playing Erin Brinkley because of the explosions. The explosions were really awesome."

Marion shook her head.

"What, like you've never enjoyed the spectacle?" Jess challenged her.

It made Marion grit her teeth. "I don't think my filmography involves anything that goes *boom*, no."

"I didn't say anything about things going *boom*. I believe I said *spectacle*. You can't tell me you didn't do that nude scene because you knew it would create a stir."

"I haven't any idea what you're talking about." Of course, that wasn't why she had done it. Well, that hadn't been the only reason. The script had called for it and she had believed it was necessary. That it would make Tabitha furious had been a bonus. The press reaction had been an afterthought.

"You never do, do you?" Jess retorted. Marion flinched at the reminder of the last real conversation they had engaged in when they were younger.

The rest of the cast shifted uncomfortably in their seats. She couldn't help it. For good or ill, Jess still knew how to get under her skin. When they had been younger, it led to nights Marion would never forget. Now, Jess could cause greater wounds than she likely realized. "If you'll excuse me." She looked pointedly at Jess before standing and heading toward the restroom. If she was going to spend the rest of the night deflecting Jess's barbs, she needed a moment to compose herself first.

Standing in the bathroom, Marion looked at her own reflection in the mirror. She wished she knew how to reduce the tension between herself and Jess. Despite any hopes she might have, they might never be more than colleagues, and that was fine, but they needed to call a truce. Too bad Marion didn't know how to establish one. Would talking about the past really help? Or would it just make things that much worse? She didn't know. Was she willing to take that risk? She wasn't certain.

By the time Marion came back to the table, the conversation had moved on to a different topic, Jess had found a new seat down by Jewel, and Lauren was nowhere to be seen.

Marion took a moment to look around the bar to see if she could figure out why Gwen had chosen it for their night out. That's when she spotted Lauren. She was at the bar. She tossed back a shot of something, then grabbed the bartender by her vest and left a sloppy kiss on her cheek.

From there, Marion watched as Lauren allowed the woman standing next to her to tug her toward the dance floor. Lauren wrapped her arms around the woman and pulled her into a kiss as they started to move together.

Glad she was no longer so young and impetuous, Marion could only shake her head as she slid back into her seat. Still, the freedom Lauren had was enviable. What would she have done with that freedom when she was younger?

As soon as she sat down, Jess popped up, making an excuse to Gwen and Richard about going to the bar for a drink. Marion watched her go, watched her pull up a barstool and settle onto it, clearly ready to ignore her companions for a few minutes.

"I hadn't realized things between you and Jess were quite so awkward." Gwen finished her wine.

Marion looked uncomfortably at Richard. She had no desire to talk about this in front of the director even though he didn't particularly seem to be paying attention. Following Marion's glance, Gwen caught on.

"Richard, darling, would you go get me another wine?" She pushed her empty glass toward him.

"Of course." Richard drifted away from the table toward the bar and Jess.

Marion watched him go with trepidation. Gwen would want answers and she didn't have any to give.

"Now, what on Earth did you do to that young woman?" Gwen looked at Marion sternly.

"I told you we had a past. Things didn't go well and I've no desire to get into it, particularly not here." Marion motioned to the bar around them. It had filled up and there were far too many ears nearby, not to mention that any of her colleagues could return at any minute.

"Well, maybe if you apologized." Gwen offered.

"We are far beyond simple apologies and I would thank you not to discuss it further." Marion scowled. What she had done to Jess wasn't forgivable. She couldn't forgive herself. How could she expect anything more from Jess?

Richard slid back into his seat with Gwen's fresh glass of wine, cutting off any possible response.

Jess returned a moment later, too polite to ignore her hostess entirely though she didn't look at Marion.

"So, Gwen, Richard. A little birdie told me that you two used to be quite the item," Jess said.

Gwen tittered and rubbed a cheek. "That was ages ago. Wasn't it, Richard?" She reached out and squeezed Richard's hand.

"Indeed, it was. Nineteen seventy-three, I think. One of the best years of my life, even though things didn't work out." He smiled gently at Gwen. Gwen squeezed his hand again before letting go.

"We're the best of friends, now." Gwen beamed. "I can't think of anyone else I'd rather do this project with."

"The feeling is mutual." Richard sipped his cocktail. Marion was glad the turn in conversation didn't necessitate her talking to Jess. Nothing good would come of that.

"I'm a proponent of putting things in the past. You never know how giving someone a second chance might reward you." Gwen looked between Marion and Jess. Marion shifted uncomfortably.

"I tend to agree, but it's harder to forgive some things than others. Just saying you're sorry isn't enough without changed behavior." Jess shot a look at Marion as if Marion needed the confirmation that Jess was talking about her.

"Oh, nonsense." Gwen waved a hand. "Short of committing a crime, there's nothing we can't move on from."

Not able to meet Gwen's eyes, Marion looked over toward the bar.

The twentysomethings seemed to be having fun, but Lauren was pressed up against the bar with two men crowding into her space. It looked like Lauren was trying to get between them to walk away, but they kept closing in on her.

Finally, Marion couldn't let things lie any longer. She murmured something to Gwen about being right back and headed toward Lauren and the two miscreants holding her hostage. Once she got close enough, she tapped one of them on the shoulder. He turned and sneered at her.

"What d'ya want, lady?" he spat out.

"I want you to leave the young woman alone." Marion kept her voice cool. She didn't want to escalate the situation, but she was determined to get the men to leave.

"I don't need your help," Lauren mumbled from somewhere between them.

"Like she said, lady, she doesn't need your help." With a hand to her shoulder, he pushed Marion away from them.

"What's going on here?" Jess was suddenly standing at Marion's side between her and the two looming men. Jess put a protective hand on Marion's upper arm and Marion's eyes went wide with surprise and confusion. She was there to protect Lauren. Wasn't Jess there to do the same?

"These gentlemen, and I use the term loosely, are harassing Lauren. I am making them desist."

"You're doing jack-shit, bitch." The man stepped closer to Marion, stopped only by Jess's hand, which was now on his chest.

"I wouldn't do that if I were you." Jess pushed back against the man and pulled out her phone, quickly taking a picture of him before he could react. "In case you don't recognize me, I'm Jess Carmichael and I have a few million twitter followers. Unless you want every single one of them to see a picture of you with the caption *sexual harasser*, I would walk away."

For a moment, the man looked like he would chance it anyway, whether because he didn't believe Jess was who she said she was, or he simply didn't care, when Jess's bodyguard slid up behind them.

"Is this man bothering you, Ms. Carmichael?" He didn't bother to keep his voice down. If anything, he made himself look bigger.

"Oh, no. I think he's decided he's done for the night. I don't think he's going to be any more trouble." Jess met the man's eyes and didn't back down.

The man finally stepped back. "Fuck you, you bitch," he shot over his shoulder as he retreated, taking his buddy with him. As soon as he was gone, Marion turned to Lauren.

"Are you okay?" Marion looked at Lauren in concern.

"I'm fine." Lauren wrapped her arms around herself protectively. "I had it handled." She tried to push past Marion, Jess, and the bodyguard, but stumbled forward. Jess's bodyguard caught her before she could fall. Marion could tell now just how much Lauren had had to drink and it was far too much. The bodyguard gently steadied her as Jess looked over at Marion. They shared a brief moment of eye contact and jointly made a decision.

"Let's get you home." Jess rubbed Lauren's arm as Lauren seemed to deflate.

"Okay." Lauren nodded, but still didn't seem steady on her feet. Jess looked at her bodyguard.

"Go get the car. We'll take care of her." He nodded and disappeared out of the main entrance of the bar. A quick word later, and a helpful server was showing them out a side door. Marion and Jess maneuvered Lauren outside and into Jess's SUV. Just as she was about to turn and leave, content that Jess would make sure Lauren got home in one piece, Lauren grabbed her hand and tugged on it. Seeing no other option, Marion climbed into the SUV and let Lauren cling to her.

Lauren slurred her way through her address when Jess's bodyguard asked her for it, then seemed to pass out, head resting against Marion's upper arm. Jess got into the other side of the SUV and made sure Lauren's seat belt was buckled before settling down next to her.

Silence reigned in the SUV as they navigated the streets to Lauren's apartment. Marion didn't know what to say to Jess, what sort of conversation they could have that might be overheard by Jess's bodyguard and Lauren.

"I hope this is just a phase." Jess looked at where Lauren was curled up between them.

"Quite," Marion replied.

"I remember when I was her age, getting into too much trouble for all the wrong reasons," Jess said softly.

"I never had that luxury." Marion knew she sounded stiff, but she didn't know how to navigate what was going on between her and Jess. One minute they had been trading barbs and the next, they had seamlessly worked together to get Lauren out of the bar. It was confusing.

"Yes, but you were making other mistakes at twenty-five, weren't you?" Marion winced. Jess wasn't pulling her punches.

Marion looked down at her hands. "Yes. I did things then that I've regretted ever since."

Jess huffed and shook her head. "Was it really that bad? I don't remember forcing you to do anything."

"I didn't…" Marion took a deep breath. "I never said you forced me into anything. I wasn't talking about you." Despite everything, she didn't regret the short amount of time she and Jess had spent together.

"If it wasn't about me, then who was it about?" Jess bit back.

"No one. Nothing. It isn't important now." Marion waved a hand in dismissal.

"Of course not. God forbid you actually communicate with someone." Jess rolled her eyes and shifted back into her seat.

"Maybe we should just stop talking."

"That's what you're best at." Jess snipped back.

"You have no idea what you're talking about."

"Because you never gave me one. You just…" Jess made an indistinct sound and threw up her hands.

Marion wanted the night to be over. She was ready to retreat back to her own house.

"Tabitha," she said, all of the fight suddenly gone from her. "That's who I meant. I should have fired her as soon as I came of age." She shook her head and looked down at Lauren resting against her shoulder. "She wasn't good for me. The parts she got me weren't worth it. She forced me to hide so much of myself to be the perfect blank canvas for whichever director she wanted me to work with. I barely knew who I was." She looked straight ahead at the headrest in front of her. "She made me feel like I would be worthless without her."

Jess went quiet. After a moment, Marion finally looked up at Jess. She saw sympathy in Jess's eyes. A sympathy she didn't deserve. Not after everything she had done to Jess.

"I didn't know," Jess said.

"I didn't want you to." Marion shook her head. "There were reasons why I stayed with her. Some of them were even good reasons. But I wouldn't wish it on anyone else. Lauren—" She brushed some of the girl's hair back. "At least she's getting the chance to figure out who she is."

This wasn't the time or place to explain the rest. She didn't think that time would ever occur. She would always regret what she had done to Jess, but would an apology, an explanation, even work now? Tabitha had caused so much pain. It seemed she was still causing it. For both her and Jess.

Jess didn't say anything in response, and silence filled the space between them until they pulled up in front of Lauren's apartment. Marion opened her door as soon as the SUV stopped moving. She gently woke Lauren and got her out of the SUV. She looked over Lauren's shoulder at Jess. "I'll take care of her and get an Uber home."

Lauren was doing her best to pull her keys out.

"Are you sure?" Jess asked. She looked ready to hop out of the SUV, her hand already on her seat belt. "I don't mind. We could wait and give you a ride home."

"We'll be fine." Marion put an arm around Lauren's waist and guided her toward the door.

"You're sure?" Jess sounded worried.

"I'm sure." Marion got Lauren's door unlocked and pushed it open. "Go home, Jess. I'm going to stay here for a bit to make sure she's all right. There's no sense in both of us being awake half the night."

"Okay." Jess and Marion shared another look before Jess closed the SUV door. Marion turned back around to usher Lauren inside. She heard the SUV drive off behind her.

❖

1997

Morning light cut through the window at Jess's apartment. Marion winced as it made her head pound. She'd been at another party the night before, a party she had known ahead of time that Jess would be attending. It had been easy enough to slip out with her at the end of the night.

Marion raised the coffee mug to her lips and took a sip. Her cab would be there any minute and she needed to mention something to Jess. At least, she thought she should mention it. It wouldn't have mattered if she had just snuck out, but something about staying meant she needed to say something.

"What?" Jess blew on her own coffee to cool it down. She was still in her robe, though Marion was dressed to leave. "What's on your mind?"

Marion took another sip, letting the hot liquid loosen her tongue. "I'm doing a play in London. We go into rehearsals next week."

"Ah. And you thought I might be upset?" Jess got up and walked over to Marion, sliding onto her lap. "I wasn't lying when I said I knew what we were doing. I'm not expecting a commitment ceremony on the beach. It isn't even like either of us is planning on coming out. At least, I'm not anytime soon."

Jess ran her fingers through Marion's still damp hair. "I appreciate that you were concerned, though. It's very sweet of you." She leaned in and kissed Marion. "But I'm not going to go charging off after you, trying to stop you from getting on that plane. That wouldn't serve either of us."

"Good." Marion wasn't sure how she felt about Jess's speech, but that was the only possible reaction. Jess melded their lips together before Marion could think too hard. After a long kiss, she pulled away and started kissing her way down Marion's neck.

"How long do we have?" Jess asked against Marion's skin, nipping at it to punctuate her question.

"Minutes." Marion shuddered at the feeling of Jess's teeth nibbling down her neck. Jess took one of Marion's hands and placed it on her thigh, encouraging her to touch it. Marion didn't need prompting, she reached under Jess's robe and held her hip, pulling her in tighter. It was nothing to then untie Jess's robe completely and part it so she could cup one of Jess's breasts. Jess sucked in a breath and bit down harder on the curve of Marion's neck. Marion wasn't sure how she'd explain the mark if asked. She'd just have to make sure she wasn't asked.

Marion was just about to lean in and catch Jess's nipple between her lips when there was a honk outside. Marion groaned and looked over toward the door.

"That's likely for me." She reluctantly pushed Jess off of her lap before standing and wiped her hands on her slacks. "Thank you for the coffee. I suppose I'll be seeing you." She offered Jess a tight smile.

"You're welcome." Jess walked Marion to the door. She leaned in and placed a kiss on Marion's cheek before opening it. Marion gave Jess one last look before she stepped outside into the hot California sun and headed toward the taxi, unaccountably unsettled.

Chapter Six

Present Day

Marion stood in front of the door to the recording studio and took a deep breath. She had recorded most of her lines the day before. Everything had gone smoothly, though she knew she would be back in the studio eventually to rerecord some things once they were further along in the animation process. That was just how these things worked.

But, of course, they hadn't recorded everything. She still had to record her lines with Jess. She understood Richard's reasoning, but she wasn't sure if it would work as well as he hoped it would. Still, there was a reason they called her one of the finest actresses of her age, and she had been put through things far more unpleasant than an awkward afternoon for the sake of a film. Four a.m. calls, only to stand in the rain for hours, easily came to mind. Still, she'd won her second Oscar for the role that had called for that, so she couldn't complain too much.

Of course, that didn't mean she was looking forward to spending the afternoon with her ex. Funny, she had never thought of Jess in exactly those terms before. As a past lover, certainly, but Jess had never really been her girlfriend or partner or whatever the term currently in vogue was. For decades, she had tried not to think of Jess at all, and for the most part, it had worked. This was just one afternoon. She could deal with one afternoon, this one project, and then go back to pretending Jess didn't exist.

God, why had she told Jess about Tabitha? She'd never told anyone about just how tightly Tabitha had controlled her life. And to tell Jess of all people. Marion had told her something so personal, something that was such a source of shame. She shouldn't have let Tabitha control her life for so long, to force her to live the life Tabitha had wanted for her, instead of the life she had wanted for herself. She should have been stronger. If only she hadn't cared so much about keeping Tabitha happy. If only she hadn't been such a coward. If only she had stood up to Tabitha before she had met Jess, things might be different. Even if they hadn't lasted, they might be the sort of friends Gwen and Richard were today.

Still, she could get through one day with Jess. She would get to the studio early, take a few moments to center herself, and then be good for the day. All she had to do was walk in the door.

With a firm tug on the door's handle, she stepped into the outer room only to pull up short. She found Jess sitting on a low couch just inside the doorway, shoes off, legs crossed underneath her, and reading glasses on as she looked down at the script in her lap. At least, she had been looking down. Now she was looking up at Marion in mild surprise.

"Marion." Jess recovered first. She dropped her feet back to the floor and slipped her shoes back on, looking a bit embarrassed. She wore a gauzy silk top, the ombre taking it from opaque at the top to translucent at the bottom. Marion couldn't stop herself from noticing the colorful tattoos that covered Jess's ribs. Those hadn't been there before.

"Jess." Marion pulled her eyes up hoping that Jess hadn't noticed where she had been looking. She nodded in acknowledgement. She could be polite. She walked over to one of the chairs and sat, back straight and hands on her lap over her own copy of the script. Where Jess's looked tattered and covered in marker, her own copy was almost as pristine as the day it had been given to her, her parts tabbed and highlighted, notes written in a neat hand in the margins.

Margaret had been right. The scenes with Hestia and Penelope's reunion were fraught with a subtext that could easily be seen as romantic if played a certain way. But it would only work if both the actors involved played it the same way, and she and Jess weren't exactly communicating. Marion hoped Richard knew what he was doing putting them both in a recording booth at the same time.

In the time it had taken Marion to settle, Jess had gone back to her script, mouthing lines to herself. It looked like she was emphasizing different words each time she ran through them and shaking her head at each variation.

Marion tried not to pay attention to her and opened her own script, but she already had both her and Jess's lines memorized. Finally, Marion could ignore her no longer.

"Do you want to run through them?" Her voice cut through Jess's mutterings and Jess startled.

"What?" Jess blinked at Marion as if she couldn't quite believe what she was hearing.

"Our lines. Would you like to run through them before Richard arrives?" Marion offered. She would have done the same with any other colleague. Jess shouldn't be any different. And Richard was notoriously late for things, so they had the time.

"Oh." Jess still looked taken aback and wary. "I—Okay." She moved toward the end of the couch nearer Marion's chair. The sudden change in proximity made Marion's breath catch in her chest. She could smell Jess's perfume now, still floral but not as light as it used to be. A sudden longing gripped Marion. She wanted to reach out, she wanted the tension between them to go away. Maybe she *should* apologize, explain what had happened, explain how it had all been to help Jess. Would Jess even believe her? There was no way to know without saying something. She started to say something only to be cut off.

"Is something wrong?" Jess asked.

"No." Marion cleared her throat. "Nothing. We should—" She looked down at her script and then back up at Jess.

"Right. You're right." Jess nodded and turned her script to the same page as Marion before they began.

❖

"It's been…" Jess said forlornly. She looked at Marion just as sadly.

"Thirty years. Yes, I know." Marion pursed her lips. She shifted her stance in front of the microphone a bit.

"Can't we just…can't we just put it all behind us?" If Marion had harbored any doubts about Jess's ability to act, they were gone now. Jess really did sound like she wanted to put the last twenty years behind them. No, that wasn't right. It was thirty years. The characters, once childhood best friends, had been estranged for thirty years.

"Penelope, it isn't that simple." Marion rubbed her forehead.

"Why can't it be?" Jess pleaded with Marion. Penelope pleaded with Hestia.

Marion sighed. "You're right, Pen. It can be that simple. We can make it that simple." In her script, Hestia moved to pull Penelope into a hug. Obviously, Marion couldn't do that in real life. She wasn't reconciling with Jess. There would be no hugs. Still, part of Marion wanted that, wanted to be able to have an easy relationship with Jess once again.

Where had that thought come from? Marion was sure the surprise must have shown on her face and she was taken further off guard when Richard said, "Cut!"

It came over the headphones from the production booth. It took Marion a minute to recover her senses.

"That was excellent, ladies. I think that take was the one." Richard gave them a big, double thumbs-up through the glass.

Jess's entire body seemed to relax as she took off her headphones. "Phew," she said as she shook out her hands then took off her glasses. "That was exhausting. I don't know how you do it for months on end."

"It's rarely quite that long." Marion folded her script closed and stepped back from the microphone as she tried to let the energy from the scene bleed out of her.

"Really? I distinctly remember you being in a play that ran for at least four months, and that didn't include rehearsal time." Then, as if just realizing what she had said, Jess blushed and looked away. "That is—Well, isn't that how long plays normally last?" Jess looked down at her hands and then back up.

"Five to six." Marion swallowed and stood up straighter. "West End plays normally run five to six months."

"Right." Jess smiled tightly as she opened the door to the recording booth and walked out of the small room, Marion following behind her. "I must have, well…" Jess wrung her hands together. "I suppose I'll be seeing you later."

Marion let Jess leave the booth before she followed a few moments later. She was just opening the door to leave the production area when Richard looked up from his notes.

"Marion?"

"Yes?" She dropped her hand and turned to look at him. She thought they were finished for the day, but apparently Richard needed something else from her, though she couldn't guess what it might be.

"When Lauren came in to record her part yesterday, she wasn't quite connecting with it. Would you mind terribly staying and recording her scenes with her? I know I only asked you to record with Jess, but well, you did such a good job, and I'm quite pleased with how things have come out."

Marion sighed. Did all of her colleagues need hand-holding? Still, she quickly reviewed her schedule in her mind. There was nothing that couldn't be pushed off until later.

"All right. I'll stay." With one hand on her hip, Marion rubbed her forehead. "When is she coming in?"

"Soon. Why don't you hang out in the lounge and I'll have someone come get you?" Richard smiled at her, pleased that she had agreed.

"All right." Marion nodded. "I'll be around." She turned and headed out of the production booth.

❖

Marion wandered through the hallways of the studio with no real destination in mind. She wasn't exactly sure when Lauren was supposed to be there, but she didn't have anything to otherwise occupy her time. Stretching her legs seemed preferable to staring at her phone while she waited.

She was just rounding a corner when Jess came out of one of the doors that lined the hallway. She looked up and caught Marion's eye.

"You're still here?" Jess tilted her head in question.

"Yes." Marion clasped her hands together. "Richard asked me to go through Lauren's lines with her. I'm just waiting for her to arrive."

"Ah. Right." Jess crossed her arms. She looked down at her shoes then back up.

"Well, I—"

"Do you want—"

They both stuttered to a stop. Jess blushed. Marion waited for her to say something.

"Would you go on a walk with me?" Jess asked. "Just around the block or something?"

"All right." Marion didn't see any harm. They seemed to have reached some sort of détente, and in the grand scheme, a walk couldn't possibly make things worse.

"Good." Jess nodded. "Just let me grab my things." Jess disappeared back into the room and reappeared with her jacket. "Okay, I'm ready."

They walked silently to the doors to the studio then suddenly they were on the sidewalk outside. The breeze blew across Marion's face and she pulled her own jacket closer around her shoulders.

They moved slowly down the street, the silence building between them.

"So, a walk?" Marion asked. She was confused by the invitation but was willing to see what Jess really wanted.

"Mm-hmm."

"Are we walking somewhere specific?" Marion asked after a few minutes of silent progress.

"Like I said, just around the block or something, so not particularly, I guess." Jess shrugged.

"Was there something you wanted to talk about?" Marion prodded her.

"I just wanted to say I'm sorry about the other night. I jumped to conclusions and I shouldn't have. And I'm sorry about how I acted when we got coffee the other day."

Marion stopped walking. She didn't know what to say to that. She didn't know what to do. Jess took a few more steps then stopped to look back at Marion. Clearly, Marion needed to say something, or things would get unbearably awkward.

"I appreciate that." She pulled her jacket more tightly around herself. She knew that she should offer her own apology, but it rang hollow to her ears. Still, it was worth trying. "Jess, I *am* sorry about how things happened. How they ended. I know I caused you a great deal of pain." She had once had reasons for ending things the way she did, but they didn't seem like good reasons anymore, not in the face of Jess's hurt, which she hadn't given herself the opportunity to empathize with at the time. She looked at Jess, waiting with anticipation for how Jess would respond.

"I…" Jess visibly swallowed. "Thank you." She looked at Marion searchingly. "I don't know what else to say. I… thank you."

Jess's cheeks had been turned pink by the breeze, and it struck Marion just how attractive Jess was, how other people might see her, people without all of the weight of their shared history. What would it be like if their first meeting had been just a week or two ago? Would they get along? Or would they still have been at each other's throats?

Jess started walking again and Marion had no choice but to follow her. She drew up beside Jess as they turned the corner of the block back to the studio. Jess pulled the keys for her car out of her jacket pocket.

"I'm glad we could talk about this, about everything. I don't want anything to interfere with our working relationship." Jess stopped just at the edge of the parking lot.

"I don't want that either." It was best if they could just be professionals, without twenty years of emotions filling up the space between them.

"Good. Good then." Jess nodded. "I'll see you in a few days when we have that interview."

"Yes." Marion stood in front of the door to the studio.

"Well, bye." Jess gave her a little wave before she turned toward her car and got in. Marion stood where she was until Jess drove off. Would her apology change anything? She didn't know, but she could hope it did. If nothing else, she could say that she'd done it, that she'd tried. She took a deep breath of the brisk air before she opened the door to the studio and went back inside.

❖

Marion and Richard both looked up as the door to the production booth opened and Lauren shuffled inside. She still had her mirrored sunglasses on, and her flannel shirt was rumpled.

"Ah good, you're here." Richard muttered as he stood up. They had been waiting for Lauren for the last twenty minutes, and now that she had finally shown up, Marion couldn't say she was particularly impressed.

"Shall we get started?" Richard looked at Lauren pointedly. "Marion, I believe you already know the drill."

"Certainly." Marion headed to the recording booth, Lauren slouching behind her. Once they got into the booth, Lauren pulled her script from her messenger bag and placed it on a music stand. She finally took her sunglasses off, groaning quietly. Still, she had the good grace to blush at her obviously hungover state when she looked over at Marion.

"So, we just put on the headphones and go?" Lauren asked.

"That sums it up, yes." Marion took the pair of headphones resting in front of her and slipped them over her ears. Lauren nodded and did the same.

"If you ladies are ready?" Richard's voice came through the headphones. Marion looked through the various panes of glass and nodded.

"Excellent. We'll take it from scene six." Richard nodded toward a technician who began the recording.

❖

Marion looked across the recording booth at Lauren as she said her next line. "That is neither here nor there." Marion shook her head. Lauren huffed but it wasn't convincing. Richard's "cut," rang out between them, frustration obvious in his voice. Lauren stepped back from the microphone and ripped off her headphones.

"I'm just—I'm not getting it." Lauren looked like she was going to punch the music stand that held her script. She pushed it away and it teetered, clattering on two legs on the verge of falling over. Only Marion reaching out a hand kept it upright. Suddenly, Lauren looked like she was about to start crying. "I just—I need a few minutes," she said before she fled the room.

Richard flopped back into his chair, hands thrown up in exasperation as he watched Lauren leave. "I don't know what's wrong with her, but this isn't why I cast her."

"You cast her because she's an up-and-coming star with name recognition." Marion rolled her eyes. Still, from the bit of research she'd done on her co-star, she had a reputation for professionalism, not hysterics. "I'll go talk to her." She took off her own headphones and exited the recording booth, trying to figure out where Lauren might have gone off to. After checking the lounge and a few empty rooms, Marion finally caught sight of her through the sleek glass doors that led out of the studio.

Marion strode outside and looked down at where Lauren was sitting on the curb, her knees drawn up to her chest. Marion cast a thin shadow over her, but it was enough for Lauren to quickly wipe her eyes and furtively look up. She made a distressed sound and looked back at her knees.

Seeing no other choice, Marion slowly lowered herself down to the sun-warmed concrete of the curb next to Lauren. Her knees protested, but she ignored them.

"Dare I ask what's wrong?" Marion faced forward, not wanting to put the pressure of her undivided attention on Lauren. She hoped it wasn't just the hangover.

Lauren sniffed. "I'm not normally like this. I know I keep saying that, but I'm not." She tightened her grip on her legs drawing them farther in. "I memorized my lines. I rehearsed. I did everything I was supposed to do, but I just can't today." She buried her face between her knees.

"And why, pray tell, is today different than any other day." Marion did look at Lauren then. She was willing to take Lauren at her word for now, that this day really was an anomaly. Still, she wondered what her explanation would be.

"Um." Lauren finally looked up, turning to study Marion. Marion didn't know what she was looking for, but she must have passed the test because Lauren decided to speak.

"How did your parents take it?" Lauren asked.

"Take what?"

"Finding out you're gay."

Marion rocked back, not expecting the turn in conversation. Certainly, it was an open secret that she preferred women, but she wasn't used to having to talk about it. Very few people would feel comfortable asking her something so personal, but Lauren seemed to have no qualms about it. Or perhaps she needed an answer so badly she had managed to overcome the barrier that Marion normally kept around herself. How on earth was she going to answer Lauren's question?

"I'm afraid my parents and I didn't have much of a relationship. I would have been a disappointment no matter what I did." An answer that wasn't much of an answer. She had rarely seen her parents growing up, most of her care being foisted off on her agent. Tabitha had practically raised her. And when Tabitha had found out, well that reaction didn't bear dwelling on. It was nothing she wanted to share with Lauren. Not when Lauren was clearly feeling vulnerable.

"I told my parents. Last night." Lauren shook her head. "My dad took it fine, I guess. My mom though, she begged me to take it back. She started crying and I started crying and I couldn't listen to her telling me it wasn't true, that I didn't know what I was talking about. I tried to just go out and forget about it, but I just ended up sad and drunk instead of just sad."

"I'm sorry." Marion might have avoided that particular experience, but Lauren was clearly hurting, and Marion could empathize with that. She tentatively reached out and with hesitant movements, put a hand on Lauren's shoulder. "I'm sorry that happened to you."

"I just thought that they, that she, would be different. That she would be cool with it." Lauren shook her head. "I couldn't sleep last night, and I've been so awful today that I'm sure they're dying to fire me." Lauren wiped away the tears that had started to fall again.

Marion nodded and squeezed Lauren's shoulder. "I'll go tell Richard that we're finished for the day and we'll reschedule. If he has a problem with that, he can take it up with me. Do you need me to call you a car?"

"No." Lauren's voice shook. "I drove in. I can drive myself home." She wiped her hands on her thighs and prepared to stand up.

"If you're certain?" Marion followed Lauren onto her feet.

Lauren nodded. "Yeah. Thank you though. Thanks for the talk. I think I just needed to tell someone who would understand."

"Of course. If you need anything else, let me know. I'll make sure my assistant gets you my number."

Lauren's eyes went wide at the offer. "That's, you don't have to, I'm sure I'll be fine."

"Of course, I don't have to. But I'll do it anyway. Go get your things and I'll go talk to Richard." Marion rubbed the top of Lauren's arm before stepping away and striding back into the studio.

❖

Marion found Richard right where she had left him, sitting in the production booth going through a script. He looked up when she came in the door. "Did you find her?" He looked resigned to the answer being no.

"We had a discussion. I think it would be best for us to reschedule." Marion crossed her arms. As she'd already sent Lauren home, Richard really had no choice in the matter.

"Rescheduling is going to put us over budget. I only have so much studio time blocked out." Richard shook his head.

"Don't worry about your budget. I can afford another day in the studio. That's why Gwen asked me to executive produce, isn't it? In case something went wrong, and you needed more money." She had already committed a substantial amount of money to the film, hopefully to be recouped once it opened in theaters, and in these circumstances, she was willing to spend a bit more.

"If that's what you want, I won't tell you how to spend your money." Richard closed his script. "I'd best be getting back to my office. Tomorrow's prep work won't do itself."

Marion nodded and watched him leave. She took a seat in his abandoned chair and looked into the recording booth. Both of their scripts were still on the stands. She would see that Lauren got hers back. She hoped she had said the right things to Lauren. What did she know about coming out to anyone? It wasn't something she had ever truly done. She pushed a stray strand of hair back into place. She hoped Lauren would be all right. She would have to make sure Barbara got her contact information so that she could check on her. It seemed to be the least she could do.

❖

1997

Marion looked up at the knock on her dressing room door. She had just finished removing her stage makeup and hadn't planned on having visitors. They were well into their run, after all. The excitement of opening night, which brought out all sorts of well-wishers, was long past. She pulled her robe more tightly across her chest and called out, "Come in," turning to look at the door as it opened. She blinked in surprise when she saw Jess standing there. If Marion hadn't been expecting visitors, she certainly hadn't been expecting Jess. She tried not to gape.

"Hello," Jess said, as she peered around the door. "May I come in?"

"Certainly," Marion answered, smoothing down her robe while trying not to ask the obvious questions, like whether Jess had taken a twelve-hour flight to London just to see Marion perform.

Coming into the room, Jess pulled a bouquet of flowers out from behind her back. The violets charmed Marion in a way the usual roses wouldn't have, and she smiled.

"You didn't need to—"

"I was in town. Well, I'm on tour, well, technically I'm off tour for the next few weeks, but…" Jess waved a hand to cut off her own rambling speech before taking a breath and seeming to reset.

"I'm in town and I wanted to see the play. It seemed rude not to say hello and even worse to come empty-handed." She held out the flowers.

Marion chuckled as she stood. "You didn't need to bring anything, but the flowers are lovely." She stepped across the small space and took them from Jess's hands. It brought them closer together and Marion could smell Jess's perfume, something floral and heady, or maybe that was just the flowers. She couldn't be sure. She hesitated a moment, trying to find the answer on Jess's face, then leaned in to catch Jess's lips with her own.

She wasn't sure it was the right move. She and Jess hadn't seen each other in months. When they had last talked, they had agreed that their infatuation with each other was just that, an infatuation, something to be indulged and then forgotten about, put in the past. But Marion didn't have time to second-guess herself before Jess started kissing her back.

The kiss slowly built between them, their breathing and the crinkling of the paper wrapped around the flowers still nestled in Marion's arms the only sounds in the room. With an arm around her waist, Jess pulled Marion closer, but the flowers stopped them. Jess pulled away with a laugh.

"Right." Marion stepped back and started looking for a place to put the flowers.

"Bring them with us," Jess said as she grasped Marion's hand. Marion finally managed to lay the flowers on the vanity top.

"With us?" Marion asked in confusion.

"Unless you want me to ravish you right here," Jess said, voice dropping as she stepped into Marion's space once again.

"Ravish?" Marion meant for it to be mocking, but the squeak in her voice at the end belied that.

"Mm-hmm." Jess pushed closer forcing Marion to take a step back, then another, and another until the backs of her knees hit the small settee and she had to sit down. As soon as she did, Jess climbed on her lap and brought their lips together once again. "I thought you were magnificent, and now I want to show you."

"You're right," Marion managed to gasp out as Jess attached her lips to Marion's neck. "We should go." She weakly pushed back against Jess's hip, but Jess didn't budge. "I've a lovely flat. It isn't too far away."

"Mm-hmm." Jess kept kissing her way down the vee of Marion's chest left exposed by the robe. She started to untie it before Marion covered her hands and stilled them. Jess looked at Marion in question.

"Have you any idea how many people have likely had sex on this settee?" Marion sounded scandalized. Jess smirked.

"What's one or two more then?" Jess nuzzled against the point of Marion's collarbone before kissing it.

"That one more isn't going to be me." Marion pulled Jess's hands close, kissing each palm in turn. "My flat is barely ten minutes away. Let me get dressed and we can be there in fifteen."

Jess huffed but shifted back and stood. She reached out for Marion to offer her a hand up, which Marion took. "I'm holding you to that. Fifteen minutes or I'm going to have my way with you in a back alley."

Marion laughed before she leaned in and kissed Jess again before pulling back. "Go wait in the hallway. I'll be out in five minutes."

"Fine," Jess huffed again, rolled her eyes, and did as she was bid.

❖

"Just give me a second." Marion tried to line her key up with the door to her flat, but Jess's hands on her ribs weren't helping.

"You said fifteen minutes," Jess breathed hot into her ear. "That was eighteen minutes ago."

Marion batted away Jess's hands. They were on the top floor of the small building, barely two floors up. Any of her neighbors could come out into the hallway and see them, but Marion couldn't quite bring herself to care. Jess was soft against her back and she wanted to give herself over to that touch. She focused harder on getting the door unlocked. Finally, the key slid in and the tumblers slotted into place and they stumbled inside.

As soon as the door was shut, Jess pushed Marion up against it. They came together in a furious kiss. Marion hadn't been pining over Jess, but she found now that part of her had missed this. Not sex. She could have found that if she had wanted it. No, she had missed *Jess*. The smell of her perfume, the feel of her skin, the shape of her face under Marion's hands as she cupped Jess's jaw.

Marion tried to push forward and guide them toward her bedroom, but apparently, Jess didn't want to wait. Her hands were already at the button of Marion's trousers, unfastening them, tugging down the zipper, and then sliding her hands beneath the waistband. Marion arched forward as Jess grabbed her ass. Then, Jess moved her hand under the top edge of Marion's panties and started to push them down, taking Marion's trousers with them. Jess dropped to her knees.

"I can't believe it's been five months since I've gotten to do this," Jess said in hushed tones as she ran her hands up Marion's thighs. She got to the apex and kept going, spreading Marion's lips, then leaning in and taking a deep breath. Marion stared down at Jess's head, anticipating her next move. When Jess hesitated a moment longer, Marion whined.

Jess's eyes shot up and they made eye contact. The contact held as Jess finally leaned forward. Marion jumped when Jess's tongue made contact with her clit, but Jess's hands kept her in place.

The warmth of Jess's mouth made her groan as Jess swirled her tongue over Marion's clit. Marion's hips rocked forward and backward as she sought out more contact with Jess's tongue. They moved together as Marion tried to find purchase on the door with her hands. Her quest proved futile, and her nails merely scraped against it.

When she came, it was nearly out of nowhere, quick and hard and knee-shaking. It was almost embarrassing just how little effort Jess had put forth to make it happen. Marion slid down the door, shivering as her back came into contact with the cool wood. She ended up on her knees in front of Jess, reaching to pull her into a hard kiss. She could taste herself on Jess's lips and it only spurred her on.

Marion pushed forward until Jess was forced onto her hip and then onto her back, Marion hovering above her.

"Didn't you say something about a bed?" Jess wrapped her arms around Marion to keep her close.

"The bed can wait." With no preamble, Marion put her hand under the bottom of Jess's skirt, her forearm pushing it up even as Marion pulled Jess's underwear to the side. She ran her fingers through the already collecting wetness.

Jess gasped. "You're right. Who needs a bed?" She cupped Marion's jaw and pulled her into another, deeper kiss.

❖

"I've been thinking about you." Jess trailed her fingers over the small of Marion's back. They had eventually made their way to Marion's bed, and now, stretched out on it, Marion hummed in response to Jess's declaration.

"Have you?" Marion blinked lazily. Head pillowed on her hands, she didn't think she would ever want to move again. Jess kissed the back of her shoulder.

"I know what I said. I know…" Jess shrugged helplessly. Marion rolled onto her side to look at her. She cupped the side of Jess's face and kissed her in encouragement.

"What is it?"

Jess took a deep breath. "I don't know what you want, and I know we probably don't have any sort of future, but I have a few weeks free, nearly a month, and I can't think of anywhere I'd rather be than here."

Marion felt something settle in her chest, felt something click into place. She pulled Jess forward into another kiss. "If this is where you want to be, then you're welcome." Marion nuzzled into Jess and kissed her one more time, sweet and lingering. Jess had other ideas though, and just as Marion was ending the kiss, Jess slipped her tongue into Marion's mouth and brought her hands up to her breasts, the whole affair turning hot and dirty.

"I hope you don't think I'm done with you yet." Jess growled, pushing Marion onto her back and climbing on top of her.

CHAPTER SEVEN

Present Day

Marion sighed deeply as the studio audience stopped clapping and Rebecca started her monologue. It wasn't her first time on the *Rebecca Levi Show*, but it was the first time she was nervous about it. She tapped her fingers against the arm of the couch in the green room. Rebecca was known for pulling off bonkers stunts and occasionally asking off-the-wall questions. Marion hadn't been a target in the past, but she had seen Jess's last appearance and it had involved slime. Marion shuddered in revulsion. It wasn't the possibility of slime that filled Marion with dread though. What if Jess said something, hinted at something that exposed their past relationship? There was no controlling Rebecca and there was no controlling Jess. They might start out talking about the film, but there was no predicting where they would end up.

On the other side of the room, Jess chatted with one of the PAs. She looked unconcerned that the world might find out about something they had both kept a secret for more than twenty years.

Marion tuned it all out, the monologue and Jess's conversation, and the general noise of the studio and focused on her own breathing. She pulled air into her lungs then exhaled it, hopefully exhaling her nerves with it. Her heartbeat slowly calmed.

"Marion." A hand brushed her shoulder and she startled. She opened her eyes to find Jess standing in front of her. The room had emptied out. "Sorry," Jess said sheepishly. "They're about to call us. I thought…" Jess shrugged.

"Thank—" Marion cleared her throat. "Yes, thank you." She stood and took another deep breath. She simply wouldn't let Jess and Rebecca pull them off-topic. That settled it.

❖

"So, Jess, Marion, what was your favorite thing about working with each other?" They were sitting in their respective seats now that the introductions were out of the way and the audience had quieted.

Before Marion could formulate a reply, Jess jumped in, "I'm pretty sure everyone has said this already, in fact I know everyone has said this already, but Marion brings such a truthfulness to everything she does. Even on an animated movie, she's always authentic to the character she's playing. And as someone who's never acted before, she's been incredibly helpful." Marion thought back to their disastrous coffee meeting. It made her pause. She didn't want to say the wrong thing, not here, not when she couldn't retreat if necessary.

"Yes, well." Marion shifted uncomfortably. "I have to say, Jess has tackled the challenges of acting with enthusiasm. And the music she's written suits the story superbly."

"Speaking of the music," Rebecca said, "Jess, how was writing for a movie different than writing something for one of your albums? I'd think it'd be harder. Was it harder?"

Jess laughed. "So much harder. Normally, I can just rely on my emotions in the moment to power me through a song, but I had to be much more deliberate with this project. There isn't really a call for a heartbreaking ballad in a movie aimed primarily at children." She laughed, and the audience laughed with her.

Rebecca turned to Marion. "Do you do any singing in the movie? What was that like?"

"I do a bit of singing, though we haven't recorded anything yet. I'm only the slightest bit apprehensive. I've never had to sing in a film before, so it's a bit of a challenge."

"I'm sure Jess will do a good job holding your hand. I hear she's good at that sort of thing." Rebecca waggled her eyebrows as she leaned into the innuendo.

Marion froze. How was she supposed to answer that? Was she supposed to pretend she didn't understand the implication? Or would it be better to respond in kind? Jess jumped in before she could figure it out.

"Oh, you know me. I'm always gentle someone's first time." Jess laughed lightly, sharing the inside joke with Rebecca and a subsection of her audience. Marion shifted uncomfortably.

"Well, I can't wait to hear your debut. And I've got one last, very important question for both of you. It's a real doozy."

"Oh, I can't wait." Jess's eyes sparkled under the studio lights as Marion sucked in a breath in apprehension. This was it. This was when Rebecca brought up something from the past that caused everything to crash down around them. Marion braced herself.

"If you could cast any spell in real life, what would it be?" Marion almost laughed in relief. That was it? That was the question Rebecca had built up to? It was preposterous.

"Well, I don't know about Marion, but as someone who has experienced several very public heart breaks," Jess laughed again, "I think a spell to show me who my true love is would be wonderful."

"I think a lot of people would want to cast that spell." Rebecca said. "What about you, Marion? Do you want to know who your true love is?"

Marion tried not to panic. It was a silly question. It didn't mean anything. Marion chuckled but sounded flat to her ears. "No. No. I think I might like some sort of invisibility spell though." She certainly wanted one just then. Anything to get out of a discussion about Jess and her true love. She wanted the interview to be over. Hadn't Rebecca said this was her last question?

"I have so many follow-up questions, but we don't have time, so I guess we'll leave it there." Rebecca turned back to the camera and teased the next segment, but Marion didn't pay attention. She closed her eyes and took a breath and prayed that the commercial break would come quickly. She could feel the beginnings of a headache already.

❖

Marion slid into the back of the town car the studio had insisted she and Jess use to get to and from the interviews. It had been a long day. A long day of pretending she and Jess were good friends. It wouldn't have done to tell Rebecca the truth: that they had only managed a tentative truce that felt like it might fall apart at the slightest challenge. Instead, they had gamely played along, the award-winning actress and the musical icon forming a tight friendship over the course of a few weeks. That was what everyone wanted to hear.

Marion closed her eyes against her headache. Then Jess's perfume filled the space as Jess sat beside her. Marion exhaled, trying to get the smell out of her nose. It didn't do any good. Even after all of these years, she didn't need the reminder to know exactly what Jess smelled like, what she smelled like even after the perfume wore off. She grabbed a bottle of water and pressed it to her temple.

"Is everything all right?" Jess asked, and for some reason the concern in her voice tipped Marion over the edge.

"The show is over. You can stop pretending now," Marion snapped then winced. She hadn't meant to be confrontational.

"I wasn't pretending!" Jess huffed. "You know what? Fine. I thought, maybe, as one person to another I might check on you because you're pale, and you look like you're in pain, but if you can't accept even that much care from me, then fine." Marion felt Jess adjust how she was sitting to get even farther away from Marion. So much for that truce.

Marion groaned and opened her eyes. "Jess," she sighed.

"No." Jess held up a hand between them. "You don't get to say *Jess* like that, in that tone. We're not bickering over where to get dinner before your next performance. You don't get to. We're not..." Jess looked away from Marion and out the window.

Marion lowered the bottle of water, looking at her hands, then at Jess, then back at her hands. She cleared her throat. "I'm sorry. I have a headache." She opened her bottle of water but closed it again without drinking any of it.

Jess shook her head. Their eyes caught and held. "I used to think you were so easy to understand. I didn't know you at all, did I?"

Marion had to look away. She finally took a sip of her water. They sat in silence. Finally, Jess spoke.

"I don't suppose you'll tell me why?" Jess asked softly. She looked up at Marion through her eyelashes, a slight frown on her lips.

Marion took a breath. "I told you—"

"You told me bullshit. We both know it. I just wasn't brave enough to call you out on it back in the nineties." Jess crossed her arms over her chest and turned more fully toward Marion only to have Marion turn away.

"It doesn't matter anymore," Marion said softly, sadly.

"It matters to me. Damn it, Marion." It seemed like Jess wasn't going to let her off the hook. How had this conversation started? How had they gotten here?

"Ask me something easier. Ask me something easier and I'll answer you," Marion pleaded as she looked down at her lap.

"Too bad that's the only thing I want to know," Jess said. She turned away from Marion again.

"I'm not doing this. Not now." Marion's voice was hard. She needed to stop this. She needed to stop this, or she would end up telling Jess everything.

"You wouldn't do it then. You won't do it now. When would be a convenient time for you, Marion? When will you tell me what the fuck happened? What happened between London and Berlin that made you leave me?" Jess's voice cracked. She hit the car door with the side of her fist and glared at Marion. There were tears in her eyes, but Marion knew she would never let them fall.

"I didn't want to leave you."

"Didn't you?"

"No, I didn't. We couldn't." Marion's voice rose. She put down her water bottle.

"Couldn't what? Have a rational conversation about it?"

"Jess—"

"No." Jess reached out and grasped Marion's forearm. "If you think you did anything other than break my heart in the most cruel way imaginable, you're rewriting history. I never did anything to deserve what you did to me."

"I never wanted—"

"Oh, you never wanted? Then why?"

"I don't want to…"

"Why, Marion?"

Marion's head spun. She couldn't handle this conversation. There were reasons why she did what she did, why she had never told Jess the truth. The air between them was too thick. The car closed in around them, full of unsaid things.

"Stop." Marion wrenched her arm away from where Jess was still holding it. "I can't do this." Jess huffed in disbelief, her cheeks reddening.

"But you can sit around all afternoon pretending to be my friend?"

"It's called acting." Marion pulled a hand through her hair.

"It's called lying."

"You were doing the same thing." Marion bit back.

"You didn't give me much choice." That one stung— the unfairness of it, as if it had been a choice of all things.

"You're impossible," Marion ground out. "I suppose it was all my fault then? And what was that ridiculous answer about *finding your true love* as you put it to that woman?"

Jess looked completely taken aback, but her surprise soon melted to outrage. "It was a silly answer to a silly question."

"Is that why you wouldn't look at me after?" Jess snorted in derision, but there was no amusement in her tone when she answered.

"Please, Marion, I gave up on the idea that you might be my true love years ago."

Marion recoiled as though she had been slapped. She felt the blood drain from her face and then just as quickly, felt it heat up, and then to her horror a lump materialized in her throat and tears pricked against her eyes. She pushed them away, but she couldn't look at Jess. She looked down at her hands instead.

"Marion?" She didn't answer.

It was one thing to imagine Jess Carmichael hating you, another thing to have her all of about three inches away telling you she did. Or what Jess had actually said, which somehow felt worse. All of a sudden, the full, tidal-wave force of devotion she had felt for Jess twenty years ago came unbidden, and Marion sucked in a breath. That deep, utter conviction that what she felt for Jess was true, and powerful, and shared. But just because Marion knew she'd never love anyone the way she had loved Jess, didn't mean there was anything to do about it now. Clearly, she had ruined things. She couldn't bring herself to meet Jess's gaze, scared of what she might find.

"I'm sorry." Marion swallowed. She looked straight ahead.

"And I need to know why," Jess pleaded.

Marion shook her head. As she turned to look out the window once again, she heard Jess sigh in resignation. The end of the car ride couldn't come soon enough.

CHAPTER EIGHT

Present Day

Music folio in hand, Marion stepped into the warmth of the recording studio once again. She tried not to think about what she was doing there. Or rather, she tried not to think about who she might have to do it with. Would Jess be there? Or would she have pawned Marion off on one of her assistants, after all? Marion's singing part was small enough that getting an assistant to cover it wouldn't be unusual.

She was a little early, so she stepped into a side room to gather her thoughts only to run into an assistant putting away equipment.

"I'm sorry, I didn't mean to—"

"No worries. You're fine." The woman smiled at her and continued with her work. The room descended into silence. "Looking forward to today?" the assistant asked over her shoulder as she shoved a box onto a rack.

Marion laughed nervously. "Not really. I'm not much of a singer." There was something freeing about actually admitting it to someone. It was easier to think her trepidation was entirely based on her ability to sing and not on who she might be singing for. The assistant looked at her curiously.

"If you don't mind me asking, if you can't sing, why did you agree to do the movie?" She went back to arranging things as she asked, only half paying attention to Marion.

"Oh, I can stay on pitch well enough. I'm just glad I don't have to carry any of the songs. Naomi is much better suited to that." Marion checked her wrist to see the time. So much for her moment of respite. "I need to get in there. It was nice talking to you."

"Yeah, you too." The assistant waved a hand in good-bye as Marion opened the door and stepped into the hallway. She did her best not to let her nervousness show on her face as another assistant smiled at her and opened the door to the production booth to usher her in.

As soon as she entered the room, she saw Jess standing by the soundboard. She had her glasses on again, and her blazer sleeves pushed up her arms and Marion sucked in a breath, attraction warring with the nervous churning in her stomach. She supposed it made sense that Jess would be there. If she had been directing her first film, she wouldn't want to give up control to an assistant no matter what her relationship with her co-workers was like. She assumed creating and producing music for your first film was much the same.

Marion stood in the doorway as they stared at each other.

"Marion." Jess smiled, but it felt brittle.

"Jess." Marion nodded. Jess's shoulders were pulled in, as if Marion might attack her, as if Marion's very presence was a threat. "Where do you want me?" It came out softer than she intended, maybe because of her nerves, maybe because of something else, some lingering need to apologize, and to tell Jess the truth.

Jess swallowed. "Just through here," she said as she opened the door to the recording studio and led Marion to a small booth. Jess followed Marion in and picked up the headphones that were draped over a music stand. "These are…" Jess fiddled with the headphones for a moment before holding them out. "These are for you."

"Thank you." Marion reached for them and their fingers brushed. Jess looked down and away, a light blush coloring her cheeks. Marion shifted on her feet. They stared at each other.

Finally, Jess exhaled, deflating as she did so. "Maybe this isn't the place, but I don't know when we might see each other again. I just need you to know that you really hurt me. What you did wasn't okay." Jess swallowed and crossed her arms and looked down.

Marion felt Jess's words in the pit of her stomach. She wanted to reach out to Jess, but she knew that Jess wouldn't appreciate the gesture. "I know. I know it wasn't." Marion worried her fingers together. What else was there to say? "It hasn't been easy these past few weeks, constantly being reminded of my worst mistake. Not you. But the way things ended." Jess looked up and met Marion's eyes. She looked as if she wanted to say something, but nothing was forthcoming.

"For what it's worth, I am sorry." She needed to say it. She needed Jess to hear it even if she didn't believe her. "I was…I was such an idiot. I know how much I hurt you, and I shouldn't have done it. There were better ways. I loved you, but…" Marion shook her head. "I would like for us to be friends, if you think that's possible."

Jess hesitantly nodded. "I appreciate that. I'll think about it, being friends."

Silence grew between them.

"We should get started." Jess finally broke the silence.

"Of course." Marion nodded. She looked at the music stand and put her copy of the score down on it. It was full of her voice coach's scribblings. Jess looked at the score and raised her eyebrows.

"Wow." She spun the stand toward herself and looked over the notes with a critical eye. It was Marion's turn to blush.

"I hired someone." Marion wrung her fingers together.

Jess smiled genuinely. "I should have known you'd be prepared." She turned the stand back around. "There's no reason for you to be nervous. I promise I'll make this as painless as possible." She reached out as if to squeeze Marion's hand. They both looked down before Jess self-consciously pulled hers away.

"You know." Jess looked up at Marion. "It's probably going to be a long day." She sighed. "Truce?" With a steeling breath, she thrust her hand out in Marion's direction.

Marion's eyes went wide as her eyebrows climbed up her forehead.

Marion carefully took Jess's hand. They hadn't touched so deliberately in twenty years and Marion did her best to ignore the way it made her feel as they touched now. There was no sense in feeling that way again. Still, she knew those hands. She *knew* those hands. "Truce."

Jess nodded and finally let go of Marion's hand.

Jess left the booth, ponytail bouncing behind her. Marion watched her as she passed through the door to the production booth, then Marion adjusted the headphones over her ears and looked down at her score.

"All right, we're going to do a few warm-ups. You just need to match your pitch to the piano, and we'll be good." Jess looked at Marion through the two layers of glass that separated them.

❖

Marion took a deep swig from her water bottle as they paused between takes. She wondered if it would be considered too diva-ish to request a cup of tea. She absently rubbed the front of her throat and arched her neck to try to dispel some of the tension gripping her body. She slipped her headphones off her ears and put them back on the stand.

The process hadn't been terrible, but it certainly seemed like more work than recording her lines had been. And Jess kept changing where she wanted Marion to breathe. They'd switched to a different key twice. It seemed like it was never going to end.

She startled when someone tapped on the door to the recording booth. She hadn't noticed him approaching. She opened the door.

"You took your headphones off before you heard." He shrugged "Anyway, we're taking a break."

"A break?" Oh, thank God.

The assistant shrugged again. "Jess takes a break, we all take a break. She's the boss, right?" He held the door open for Marion as she stepped out of the small room and into the production booth where Jess was already sipping something that smelled overpoweringly of coffee. Marion wondered if it would be possible to get that cup of tea.

Jess nodded toward a lightly steaming cup. "It's slippery elm tea. I know it isn't your preference, but it's good for your throat."

Marion took a sip and wrinkled her nose. "It's—"

"Kind of thick. Yes, I'm aware." Jess laughed lightly and perched on the arm of the couch. "Come over here and sit down. You look tense and you're supposed to be resting." She nodded toward the seat next to her.

Marion hesitated then found herself obeying. She could sit next to Jess. She could deal with that.

"You should try to get rid of some of that tension in your neck and shoulders," Jess offered. "Maybe rub them a bit?"

Marion nodded jerkily as she brought a hand up to her neck. She tried to massage away some of the knots that had formed there over the last few hours, grimacing whenever she found a sore spot.

Jess looked at her sympathetically. "You're not very good at that, are you?"

Marion winced. "Not particularly, no." Nonetheless, she kept trying to release the tension from her body.

"If you don't mind, I could…" Jess shrugged. "Just, turn around a bit and we'll see if I can't help."

"I don't see how." Marion knew what Jess wanted. She had rubbed Marion's shoulders back when they'd been racked with worry that they had been caught, that everything in her life, in their lives, was over.

"Just trust me?" Jess looked at Marion so sincerely that Marion nodded and turned around.

Marion tensed further as soon as Jess's hands touched her shoulders. Jess made a displeased noise but didn't stop. She leaned forward and murmured, "Drink your tea and relax," in Marion's ear, and suddenly Marion didn't feel anything close to relaxation. It took everything she had not to shiver at the way Jess's breath ghosted over her ear. Jess seemed unaffected as she kept digging her fingers into Marion's muscles.

Marion tried to do as she was told. She sipped her tea and submitted to Jess's hands and eventually she started to relax in spite of herself. Then Jess scraped her nails through the hair at the nape of her neck, and this time Marion couldn't stop the shiver that ran down her entire body.

Did she know that she still possessed the ability to feel this way? The rushing in her blood, the desire to drop her head forward and let Jess do what she would. It wasn't the first time they had been in this position, but Marion recalled it involving Jess's lips as a much more prominent feature. What would it feel like if Jess kissed her there now? Would it still drive her mad? She wanted to find out.

Marion gently pulled away from Jess's hands, making sure she knew that she wasn't completely rejecting her. She turned back around and looked up at Jess who seemed a bit dazed. Jess closed her eyes, staying like that for several heartbeats before she opened them again. Marion wouldn't swear to it, but she thought she caught a flash of desire reflected down at her. It made her chest constrict, forced the air out of her lungs, tightened the muscles in her throat.

Jess was not supposed to make her feel this way, unmoored and lost and wanting. The longer she sat there, the more muddled she became.

Finally, she couldn't stand it anymore. Marion stood and paced to the other end of the production booth. "I think I'm ready to start again." She put her mug down on a side table.

"Right." Jess looked up at Marion and Marion knew she wasn't the only one feeling this new pull between them. She watched Jess clench her hands as if stopping herself from reaching out again. They had tried this once and it had ended in catastrophe. Marion couldn't afford for that to happen again. She opened the door to go back to the recording booth. She just needed to get through the rest of the afternoon and then she wouldn't have to see Jess again until they started doing publicity for the film in a few months.

❖

1997

Marion startled as she felt Jess's ankle come to rest against her own under the table. There was a mischievous grin on Jess's lips as she held a finger up to them and whispered, "Shh."

Marion's eyes widened as Jess's toes curled over the top of her foot. They were waiting for their dinner to be served, but despite the early hour, the restaurant was slammed, and it was taking an unusually long time. If they didn't get their food soon, Marion would have to give up on the meal entirely in favor of getting to the theater on time.

"I'm probably going to have to go straight to the theater from here," Marion said as she looked at the watch on her wrist.

"If you must." Jess sighed an over-exaggerated sigh as she shook her head. "Whatever shall I do with myself while you're off being brilliant?"

Marion cleared her throat. "There's a key under the mat. I should have given it to you earlier, but—" She shrugged. She hadn't thought about it, she hadn't thought about Jess being anywhere other than at her side.

"Hmm. I suppose I should go get some clothes from my hotel room." Jess was still wearing what she'd had on the night before, though truthfully, they hadn't spent much of the day clothed at all.

How Jess did it, left her completely disarmed and at her mercy, Marion didn't know. She just knew that she didn't think she would ever get enough of it. Things had happened so fast. Four days in LA five months ago, and less than twenty-four hours in London, and somehow Jess had gotten under her skin in a way no one else ever had. It didn't make sense. It wasn't logical, but there she was letting Jess move into her flat for almost a month with barely a thought.

"That would probably be for the best, yes." Marion moved her cutlery around, straightening the already straight pieces. What would happen if someone found out? Would they just assume she and Jess were friends? God, she hoped so.

Jess reached for her hand, covering it with her own. Marion recoiled almost instantly, looking around the restaurant to see if anyone might have noticed.

Jess looked taken aback but folded her hands in her own lap. "Sorry. I wasn't…" Jess ran a hand through her hair, resetting it. "You make it hard to think." She shrugged.

"It's—" Marion looked down at her own hands before she met Jess's eyes. "It's fine. You make it hard too." She curled her fingers up then relaxed them. "I can't afford for anyone to know." Tabitha. She couldn't afford for Tabitha to know. Couldn't afford to have this get back to her.

"I know. I can't either," Jess said as Marion nodded. Jess's foot moved away from Marion's leg and back to her own side of the table.

Marion looked for something to say, something to break the unpleasant tension that had taken over the table. She knew she had told Jess she could stay with her for the month, but she was still uneasy about it. Things had been simple when they were in bed together. What she wanted had been clear. Now, in the light of day, she hoped that getting to have Jess close for so long was worth the risk. Before she could put her thoughts into words, their server came back with their food.

CHAPTER NINE

Present Day

Marion made her way through the crowd following the usher to her table. She'd finished recording her part for *Petunia's Potion* a few days before, and while they might still need her input as a producer, her day-to-day involvement was over, and she was currently enjoying her time off between projects. A week or two from now, she'd be itching for something to do, but for now, the time off was welcome. It allowed her to do things like this, attend Julia's annual fundraiser for the Resolve Foundation. She was picky about the events she attended, normally preferring to just write a check and be done with it, but Julia was one of her oldest friends, and she got a personal invitation every year, so she made it a point to attend. It was going to be dreadfully dull, they would make some speeches, give out some awards, a few of the kids would say something, and then there would be dancing. She was sure some of the younger attendees would find their way to whichever gay club happened to have the most hype at the moment, but she wouldn't be joining them.

Marion took her seat at the table and watched as the ballroom filled up, the seats around her quickly becoming occupied. The lights dimmed slightly as the first speaker appeared on the stage that ran the length of the front of the ballroom. As soon as she started speaking, introducing Julia, Marion tuned her out. These things had a rhythm, operated on a closely managed script. It would be at least half an hour before she needed to make small talk with the other people at her table. The seat immediately to her left was still empty, one of the few in the room, but plans changed at the last minute and Marion didn't think anything of it.

Ten minutes into the speeches, Marion caught sight of movement from the corner of her eye. She turned to see what had disturbed her and immediately closed her eyes against the sight. Jess. Her stomach swooped, though she couldn't tell if it was in dread or excitement. Their eyes caught and held. Laughter burst through the room, startling both of them into movement. Marion looked away as Jess pulled out the seat next to her and sat down. The ceremonies continued. Marion tried to pay attention. When that didn't work, she tried to zone out. No matter what she did, she could swear she felt Jess's body heat radiating off of her. She shifted in her seat trying to put some distance between them, but there was nowhere for her to go. She hoped that the speeches wouldn't last for too much longer. She wanted to find Julia, make her excuses, and leave. At the same time, she wanted to stay, wanted to know what would happen with Jess now that they seemed to be getting along. What did that moment in the studio mean? That moment when Jess was rubbing her shoulders and Marion wanted to melt into Jess's hands just as she had when they were younger. She felt like she was being torn in two directions: avoiding

Jess as best she could to prevent another fight like they had gotten into in the car, or trying to get closer, try to find out what Jess was feeling now. The conflicting impulses were making her stomach churn.

Marion took a deep breath as the lights came back up. At the very least, she could make small talk with Jess through their dinner, though she hoped their table mates would take care of most of the discussion. She didn't have to worry though. Almost as soon as the first course was served, Jess was out of her seat, and kneeling next to someone two tables over, engaged in exactly the sort of light conversation Marion could barely pull off. At the same time, she wanted Jess to stay at the table, to stay nearby.

"So, Marion." Marion turned her attention back to the woman seated opposite her at the round table, but she barely heard the woman's question. Her eyes followed Jess as she moved from one table to another. The rest of dinner proceeded in the same way. Jess would appear for a few moments as each course was served then immediately disappear again.

Marion sighed as the last of the dessert plates were taken away. She needed to mingle at least a little. If nothing else, she needed to speak with Julia and compliment her on a successful evening before she slipped out. Her driver was probably already getting ready to pick her up. She stood up and feigned casualness as she approached the area where people had started to gather. There were multiple people there that she knew. She'd start looking for them and then make her way to wherever Julia was holding court.

She was at the edge of a nearby group when someone caught her hand. She turned and found Jess looking at her sheepishly.

"Yes?" Marion said in surprise. She tugged her hand back.

"Nothing. Never mind." Jess shook her head and turned to go.

"No, Jess. I'm sorry. I was just surprised." Marion rubbed her forehead. Jess looked at her expectantly. "I didn't expect it to be you."

"It's fine. I just," Jess took a deep breath, "I feel like we're starting to get along, and despite everything, I would like to be able to count you among my friends."

Marion didn't know what to say. She had been certain she wouldn't see or speak to Jess again until the publicity tour they would do just before the film came out. Now Jess was standing in front of her asking to be her friend. She didn't know if she could take Jess up on the offer or not. She knew what she wanted to do.

She didn't get a chance to answer before Julia slid out of the crowd near them. She had a broad smile on her face as she approached.

"Two of my favorite people and I find them together. What are the odds?" Julia pulled Jess into an enthusiastic hug and Marion felt an inexplicable flash of jealousy. There was nothing for her to be jealous of. She and Jess didn't have that sort of relationship. They barely had a relationship at all. Still, a part of her that she did her best to ignore wondered what it would feel like to have Jess's arms wrapped around her again.

Julia's lips on her cheek pulled her from her thoughts. Marion returned the kiss and smiled.

"I hope you didn't mind me telling them to seat you at the same table. I know you're working together now, and we all used to be such good friends. I would have joined you if they hadn't needed me on stage. I'm sure you had more fun than I was having."

"I think Jess may have talked to everyone in the room except for the people at our table." It could have been a cutting remark, but Marion kept her tone light. Jess laughed.

"There were just so many people I needed to catch up with." Jess slid her arm around Julia's waist. Julia draped her arm over Jess's shoulders. Marion knew Julia was married, she was sure her husband was around somewhere, but Marion felt that flash of jealousy again, anyway. What did she have to be jealous about though? They were friends. They were just friends and barely that.

"You always were good at talking to everyone. I mean, you even charmed Marion here, which I thought was impossible." Julia's smile got wider as Marion blushed. "Didn't think I'd noticed that, did you?"

Marion tensed. What could she say to that? How much did Julia actually know?

"Don't worry. Whatever happened, it was twenty years ago." Julia shrugged. "And look, here we are all back together. I'm glad you've buried the hatchet though. It was terrible, having to figure out who to invite to what." Julia pulled Jess into a tighter embrace then let her go. "Anyway, as much as I'd like to stay here and reminisce, I have so many other people to talk to. The three of us must get together sometime. Lunch or drinks. Soon." She pulled Marion into a hug, which Marion stiffly returned, then hustled off and disappeared back into the crowd.

Marion could only blink after her.

"I didn't tell her," Jess said. "If that's what you're thinking."

"No. I…I may have asked if you were going to be attending some event or other one too many times. I suppose she caught on that something had happened. I don't know that I was particularly subtle." Far less subtle than she should have been, particularly with Tabitha looking over her shoulder constantly. It was a wonder she had maintained a friendship with Julia at all.

Jess huffed in amusement. She reached for Marion's hand again. "Come have a drink with me. Let's bury the hatchet for good."

Marion allowed Jess to tangle their fingers together and lead her off to the bar. They didn't speak as they walked and as they approached the bar, Jess let go of Marion's hand.

"Macallan," Jess told the bartender as she held up two fingers to indicate she wanted one for each of them. The bartender nodded and turned to look for the bottle.

"Is it still MDMA?" Marion asked as a memory came unbidden. She regretted saying it almost as soon as it passed through her lips.

"I think we've circled back around to opioids." Jess shrugged. "At least that's what the news tells me. I don't really keep up anymore." She picked up both glasses of scotch as they were placed on the bar and handed one to Marion. "I wasn't actually doing anything back then. But it seemed like a way to keep your attention." She sipped her scotch, swallowing it smoothly.

"It worked." Marion breathed in the clean, smoky smell of the scotch before she took her own sip.

"Yes, I know." A smile graced Jess's lips. It felt good, joking like this about the past, ignoring everything that came afterward. "So, what have you been up to lately? I mean, I saw you on the Oscars, but something tells me you weren't enjoying yourself, telling that terrible joke and giving that award to that stupid man."

Marion shrugged lightly. "It was my ritual sacrifice for the year. I didn't have much choice."

"God, don't you just hate that?" Jess sipped her drink. "The politics of it all. You get into it because you love it, and then suddenly there are all of these obligations that pull you away from doing the thing that you love."

"It's unfortunate, yes." Marion didn't know if she had ever loved acting the way Jess loved music. It had been something her parents wanted, and then it had been something she was good at, and now it was the only thing she had ever known. Still, she wasn't lamenting her life. She could have walked away from it all if she had wanted, but she chose to keep acting, and things had gotten much better after she had hired Margaret as her agent.

"*Unfortunate?*" Jess chuckled. "You're much more understated than you used to be." She reached out and ran her fingers over the back of Marion's hand. Marion flipped her hand over and Jess's fingertips brushed her palm. Marion wanted to close her hand around Jess's and hold it, but she didn't. She just let Jess do what she would.

"I've learned quite a few lessons in the last twenty years."

"Haven't we all?" Jess's fingers moved up to Marion's wrist. "The question is, have you learned the *right* lessons?" She drew abstract shapes on the thin skin on the inside of Marion's wrist. Marion forced herself not to react. If she drew attention to it, Jess might stop.

"I hope I have." Marion finished her scotch and subtly shook her head at the bartender when he motioned for a refill. She didn't know exactly what was happening with Jess, but she didn't want anything to cloud her thinking. "Have you?"

Jess laughed. "You're not allowed to turn my questions around on me like that." She withdrew her fingers from Marion's skin and brushed some of her own hair back. She put down her drink without drinking it. Marion wondered if the order had been a message or if Jess really had learned to like scotch in the intervening twenty years. She wasn't likely to find out that night. "God, to be twenty-three and reckless again. I remember that first night. I wanted your attention so badly." Jess shook her head.

"I remember how nervous you made me feel," Marion said.

"Really? You seemed so cool." Jess tilted her head to one side, shifting against the bar and bringing herself closer to Marion.

"Incredibly." Marion shook her head at the memory.

Jess tangled their fingers together again, looking down at where they were holding hands. "It doesn't make sense, but part of me still wants your attention." She flicked her eyes upward.

Marion licked her lips and swallowed. "You still make me incredibly nervous."

"Is that good?" Jess rubbed her thumb over Marion's knuckles.

Marion's stomach clenched at Jess's words and she made a decision. She looked around the room until she found a dark hallway. "Come with me?"

Jess nodded and Marion tugged Jess after her until they were far enough down the hallway not to be seen. Once she made sure they were hidden, she turned back to Jess. Jess looked at her, perplexed. She didn't bother answering Jess's question with words. Instead, she cupped Jess's face with one hand and pressed their lips together. Jess sucked in a breath through her nose and immediately returned the kiss. She looped her arms around Marion's neck and pulled her down. Lips brushed against lips, and the din from the ballroom faded.

Long minutes passed before they finally pulled apart.

"My place is closer," Jess whispered. She closed her eyes. Marion leaned in and placed a light kiss on her lips in reassurance. "There are still people I need to talk to before I can leave, but if you want to wait, or if you want to go over now and wait for me there?"

"If I wait here, I might lose my nerve." It was, perhaps, too honest, but it was too late now. Jess just nodded though.

"The gate code is twenty-one forty-five. There's a key under the planter on the right side of the door. Give me half an hour."

Marion kissed Jess again. "Not a minute more." She struggled to let Jess go, but after a few more kisses, she managed. With one last look over her shoulder, she left the ballroom and found her driver.

Chapter Ten

Present Day

Marion let herself into Jess's house, placing the key she had used on a table beside the door. She expected ultra-modern white leather with splashes of bright colors, likely in Jess's favorite shade of pink. A room set up more for entertaining than living. Instead, it was filled with wood and stone and a broken in leather couch in an inviting brown shade. She could picture small dinner parties taking over the generously sized table, but not the impersonal LA parties that either of them attended far too frequently.

Despite its comfort, everything in the house had an understated elegance that could only be achieved with a substantial amount of money and a good decorator. Still, it radiated Jess. Tasteful, yet vaguely erotic modern art graced one of the walls, and fresh flowers provided the colors she had expected to see everywhere.

Marion didn't know what to do with herself, but she needed to do something or all of the reasons she shouldn't be doing this would assert themselves and she would end up running. She walked through the sleek kitchen. Despite the sharp lines, the kitchen looked lived in. A stack of mail sat on the island, and there was an open bottle of wine in the fridge that Marion decided to help herself to. A quick look through the cabinets offered up a wine glass. Rosé. She smiled to herself as she poured some.

From the kitchen, she went back into the living room and took a seat on the sinfully soft leather couch. She put her glass down on the coffee table and removed her high heels. There was no point in denying why she was there. She followed that by removing her jewelry, placing it next to her wine glass. Then she picked up her wine glass again, curled her feet under herself, and tried not to overthink everything, to just exist in this space that exuded Jess. She pulled her phone from her bag and checked the time. Twenty-two minutes. She put it away.

She was halfway through her glass of wine when she heard the key in the lock and stood, turning to face the door.

Jess walked in, the sequins of her dress sparkling in the low light. Marion hadn't really been in the right frame of mind to appreciate it earlier in the night, but now that she noticed it, she couldn't look away.

"I see you found the wine." Jess toed off her shoes as she put down her bag and keys.

"I see you still favor rosé." Marion quirked a smile as she put the glass down. Jess walked into the kitchen, poured her own glass, took a sip, then abandoned it on the island as she walked over to Marion. She didn't hesitate to step into Marion's space and tilt her head up as she looped her arms around Marion's neck. She pulled Marion down into a soft kiss. Their tongues brushed together, and Marion pulled Jess closer, pulled their bodies flush. She moaned when she felt Jess's breasts push against her own.

Jess pulled away and Marion let her go. She took another step back before reaching out a hand to Marion. Marion took it.

"The bedroom is this way." Jess tugged at Marion's hand and led her up a short flight of stairs and through a doorway. Jess's bedroom opened up in front of them and Marion's breath caught in her chest. The rumpled bed invited her closer. She turned and pulled Jess back into her arms.

"Let's see what else I remember about you." She melded their lips together as she started to unzip Jess's dress.

As the last of the zipper's teeth parted, the dress fell heavily to the floor. Jess was left in next to nothing, just wisps of fabric that Marion was already looking forward to removing. Ink swooped and spiraled across Jess's skin and Marion ached to touch it all. She splayed her hand over Jess's ribs and pulled them closer together, kissing her again.

She was so distracted by touching Jess, that she was caught unawares when her own dress started to slide off, discarded and pooling on the floor. She made an indistinct noise as Jess flicked open her bra, and she let it fall as well. The kiss broke and they stood staring at each other, breath coming heavily between them.

"I hope you don't expect me to be as young as I once was." Jess smiled, her eyes sparkling.

"I should certainly hope not." Marion kissed her lightly. "I'm not exactly twenty-three anymore either."

"You're perfect." Jess twined her fingers with Marion's and pulled her closer to the bed. She pushed the covers back and got in, and Marion followed her. Marion barely had a moment to get comfortable before Jess had climbed on top of her, straddling her hips. She grinned as she leaned forward and kissed Marion again, propping herself up on one arm. "This is perfect."

As Jess started to kiss her way down Marion's chest, Marion brought her hand to Jess's hip and held on. She needed to hold on to something. Her stomach churned with nervousness as Jess nuzzled against her breast. The first time they had fallen into bed together, it was all instinct and impulse. Now, it meant more. It meant so much more.

She knew Jess's body once, but she didn't know it now. She could guess at what Jess might still like, but there was no telling if her memory was even accurate or simply embellished by time.

Marion gasped as Jess took her nipple into her mouth. Her fingers tightened against Jess's body, over a string of violets that twisted over Jess's ribs. Seeing it made Marion's breath catch in her throat. Jess stopped what she was doing and looked down at the tattoo as well. Then they both looked up and their eyes met.

"I—" Jess started to say, only for Marion to cover Jess's lips with her own. Whatever Jess was going to say, Marion didn't need to hear it. The tattoo said enough on its own. Still, part of her couldn't help worrying that it, like the first tattoos she had seen on Jess's skin, really didn't have a profound meaning. It seemed too much of a coincidence for that though. Jess wouldn't have gotten it simply because it was a pretty picture, would she?

As Jess moved on from Marion's nipple to her stomach, Marion could see the owl tattoo she remembered so well from their first encounters. Slightly faded, it still looked like it was about to launch off of her shoulder at any minute.

Then Jess spread her open and started licking her clit and Marion couldn't focus on Jess's tattoos anymore. Her thoughts turned chaotic and messy, focused entirely on what she was feeling. It felt amazing. It felt like she was about to break. She reached for one of Jess's hands and held it tightly as Jess kept licking her. She hovered at the precipice for what felt like forever before she finally crashed over, her vision going white then black.

Marion sucked in a deep breath as she came back to herself. Jess was grinning up at her from between her legs, only gloating for a second before she crawled back up Marion's body to lie beside her.

"Close enough to your memories?" Jess asked.

"Better." Marion took another deep breath before she mustered up the energy to roll over on top of Jess. "Now, I believe it's your turn."

Marion slowly came awake as a hand rubbed over her back. She took a deep breath and turned her face toward the sensation.

"I fell asleep." Marion snuggled down into the pillows before she rolled over onto her side.

"Only long enough for me to go get our wine." Jess nodded toward the nightstand where their glasses stood before she slid back into the bed. "I would tease you about it, but it's a wonder I didn't do the same thing."

Jess reached for Marion's fingers and tangled them together before lifting Marion's hand to place a fond kiss across her knuckles.

Marion sighed in contentment. "Not as young as we used to be."

"No." Jess smiled as she settled into the bed next to Marion. "But I think the sex is better." She smiled impishly.

"You're certainly more demanding than you used to be," Marion teased her. She kissed the point of Jess's shoulder even as Jess playfully shoved her away.

"I just know what I want." Jess laughed as she pillowed her head on Marion's shoulder. "Miss *I-fell-asleep-ten-seconds-after-I-orgasmed.*"

A blush spread over Marion's face and chest, but she kissed the top of Jess's head anyway. "Hand me my wine." She rolled her eyes.

"Now who's being demanding?" Jess sat up and reached for both of their glasses, holding onto them until Marion could sit up as well. Marion took her glass and took a sip. She didn't get more than one before Jess plucked the wineglass from her hand again and put both of them to the side. "Have I given you enough time to recover?" She threw a leg over Marion's and settled into her lap before pushing her fingers through Marion's disheveled hair.

"Let's find out." Marion pulled Jess down into another kiss before she toppled them both over and landed braced on her hands over Jess.

The sun was barely peeking over the horizon when Marion started to wake up, the unfamiliar bed preventing deep sleep. Jess was stretched out next to her, half on her side and half on her stomach, hand curled up on Marion's chest. She looked at peace. Marion needed to leave. She needed to get back home before anyone realized she had spent the night at Jess's. She might be far too boring for photographers to follow her around, but they did tend to trail after Jess.

"If you leave right now, I'll never speak to you again," Jess mumbled, her eyes still closed.

"It would be—"

"No." Jess pulled herself closer to Marion, molding their naked bodies together as she flung a leg across Marion's hip and pinned her down.

"Jess," Marion sighed. She put a hand on Jess's thigh but didn't push it away.

Jess cracked open one eye. "I have a plan and you're disrupting my plan." She watched Marion.

"A plan?" If Marion sounded skeptical, it was because she was.

"Mm-hmm. It involves more sex, a hot shower, and breakfast, in that order. And then I suppose you can go home. But none of those things are happening before dawn. So, get comfortable and go back to sleep for a few more hours." Jess pressed her face to the outside of Marion's arm and closed her eyes again.

"The last time you tried to make me breakfast, you nearly burned down my flat." Marion smirked, her attempt at sneaking out forgotten in the face of Jess's sleepy commands.

"That was twenty years ago. I learned how to cook."

Marion raised her eyebrows.

"I'll believe that when I see it." Marion let her own eyes start to close.

"You'll see it in two hours, now hush." Jess covered Marion's mouth with her fingers. Marion smiled against them.

"All right, you win." Marion kissed Jess's fingers and let her eyes close.

"Already knew that. Now hush." Marion didn't try to respond. She just took a deep breath and relaxed under Jess letting sleep take her once again.

❖

1997

Something was burning. Marion took a deeper breath and shot up. Something was burning. She turned around to find Jess, only Jess wasn't there, a rare situation over the past week. She stumbled out of bed and pulled on a shirt before she made her way out to the living room. The smell was coming from the kitchen. She kept going, only to hear "Shit, shit, fuck!" coming from the other room, followed by the sound of a pan clattering.

Marion finally made it into the kitchen. Jess stood in the middle of it, a slight haze of smoke in the air. She looked up at Marion with a sheepish look on her face.

"I might have burned the sausage." She looked so contrite that Marion had to laugh.

"Did you take half of the kitchen with it?" She looked around to make sure nothing was actually on fire before she pulled Jess into her arms.

"I'm sorry." Jess buried her face in the curve of Marion's shoulder. "I was trying to surprise you."

"Consider me surprised." Marion placed a kiss against Jess's temple. "Don't worry. It's just sausage."

Jess huffed. "I suppose. But now you have to let me take you to breakfast to make up for it."

"If you'd like." The thought made Marion vaguely uncomfortable, but she would do anything if it made Jess happy. Still, what if someone saw them? Or had seen them at dinner earlier in the week and put one and one together and gotten three: that she and Jess weren't just friends spending a few days together while they were in the same place. It would be disastrous.

But if Jess wanted to go to breakfast, they would go to breakfast. She supposed they couldn't spend the entire month exclusively in her flat. She smiled as brightly as she could. "Let me take a shower and we can go."

"Would you like some company in that shower?" Jess started kissing her way up Marion's neck.

"I could be persuaded." Marion ran her fingers through Jess's hair as she tilted her head to the side to give Jess greater access as she circled Jess's waist with her arms.

The smell of flowers floated through the air as Marion and Jess made their way through the open-air market. Jess flitted from stall to stall while Marion followed her at a more sedate pace. Neither of them was looking for anything specific, but they had needed to get out of Marion's flat for a little while, and the market was close enough to make it a pleasant walk.

Jess returned to Marion's side and walked next to her, their hands bumping together, but neither of them brave or foolish enough to grasp the other's hand. As they approached a flower stall, Marion touched Jess's bicep to get her to stop. Without saying a thing, she pulled out some cash and bought a bouquet of flowers. She thanked the seller and handed the bouquet to Jess.

"For you," she murmured bashfully, ducking her head before meeting Jess's eyes. Jess seemed to melt as she took the flowers from Marion.

"Thank you." Jess swallowed against something and looked like she wanted to kiss Marion. They couldn't, but Marion nodded in acknowledgement of the desire. Then Jess focused on something over Marion's shoulder. "I think our quiet afternoon is about to be interrupted."

Marion turned to see a girl of about thirteen staring at them. She sucked in a breath as Jess motioned with her head for the girl to join them.

The girl ran up to them looking adoringly at Jess. "You're Jess Carmichael, right?"

"Last I checked." Jess's laughter filled the air as she smiled down at the girl. "What's your name?"

"Uh...Alice. My name's Alice." The girl blushed. "I have tickets to your concert. My mum's taking me."

"Did you want an autograph, Alice?" Jess asked kindly. Marion tried to keep the tension from her body but it wasn't working. She was practically vibrating with it. Maybe the girl wouldn't recognize her too.

"That'd be awesome." Alice beamed.

"Cool." Jess rummaged through her purse until she found a piece of paper and a marker. A couple of quick scribbles later and Alice had her autograph, but she had attracted the attention of a number of other people walking around, recognition in their eyes. A few more brave people approached them to get autographs of their own, and Marion got relegated to photographer more than once, disposable camera after disposable camera passing through her hands.

Marion slowly relaxed as more and more people seemed oblivious to who she was. She was almost comfortable again when she heard, "Can I have your autograph as well, Miss Hargreaves?"

Marion must have stared at her for a bit too long because Alice's face started to fall. She shook herself from her daze. "Yes, certainly." Alice handed Marion the same piece of paper Jess had just signed. Marion searched her own purse for a pen when one suddenly appeared in front of her. She looked up to see Jess holding it out.

She blushed as she mumbled a "thank you," before carefully signing her name below Jess's scrawl. It wasn't the first time she had been asked for her autograph, but normally it was at the stage door after a performance. It came so rarely in public that she was always taken aback. She handed the paper back before anyone else could see, but one person was enough. If one person put it together and told the press, the tabloids would have a field day. If Tabitha found out how she was spending her time, well, it didn't bear thinking about.

She put a hand on Jess's elbow to get her attention. "We should go." She looked at Jess imploringly, and though it looked like Jess might protest, she nodded instead.

"Of course." She took back the flowers she had handed to Marion earlier, smiling at them once again, before she headed back in the direction of Marion's flat. Marion walked beside her. As far as Marion was concerned, their quiet afternoon together was ruined and her good mood along with it.

❖

"You can say it. I know you think I'm being paranoid." Marion handed Jess a glass of wine as she joined her on the couch.

"Marion, if something was going to happen, it would have happened two days ago." Jess smoothed her hand over Marion's knee.

Marion sighed. "I know you're right. I *know* you're right." She rubbed a hand over her forehead before taking a deep breath and trying to force herself to relax. "I just—"

"You worry." Jess rubbed her hand over Marion's knee. "But you don't need to worry about this anymore." She leaned in for a quickly granted kiss. "Now, come here and let me rub your shoulders and maybe you'll actually relax."

Marion sighed again but did as Jess told her to do. A second later, she felt Jess's hands on her shoulders, thumbs digging into tight knots as she sipped her wine. No one knew. If Tabitha was going to find out, she would have said something already. Just like she had in the past when Marion's friends had disappeared whenever Tabitha thought they might pose a distraction. They were safe. They had to be. Jess's fingernails scratched against the nape of her neck and sent a shiver down Marion's body.

If Jess kept touching her like that, Marion wasn't sure how long she would last. She dropped her head forward and let Jess continue the massage. Lips quickly replaced the fingers on her neck as Jess moved her hands out to her shoulders. Marion sighed in relaxation. A moment later, Jess reached around and tugged Marion's shirt off. Marion lifted her arms and twisted her head to help.

As Jess worked her way down Marion's back, Marion finally managed to stop worrying. She let the warmth of Jess's hands seep into her muscles.

"We should move this to the bed." Jess husked against Marion's skin.

Marion nodded. She slowly unfolded herself from the couch and walked to the bedroom, certain that Jess would follow her.

She felt Jess's hand on her shoulder a moment later. "Lie down." She put a little bit of force behind the touch and Marion just nodded. She sank into the bed, lying on her stomach, while Jess knelt beside her.

Jess resumed her massage with long, slow strokes over Marion's back. They didn't say much as Jess kept touching Marion. Eventually, Marion started to drift to sleep.

"C'mere," Marion mumbled as she waved Jess up to her side. Jess slid under the covers and pulled them up over Marion, snuggling into her side. Marion wrapped an arm around Jess and pulled her closer, brushing her lips against the back of Jess's neck and tangling their legs together. It was the first time they had fallen asleep without hours of sweaty sex first, and as she drifted off, Marion couldn't stop herself from wishing she could do it every night.

❖

Marion slowly came awake. Her arm was numb from the way Jess was lying on it, but she didn't want to disturb her. Instead, she rolled toward Jess, shifting just enough to restore some circulation. She tangled their legs together and Jess sighed and resettled against her. Light from the city filtered in through the curtains. What was she doing? Marion didn't know. The likelihood that they would get caught was high. Was this worth it? Marion didn't know that either, but she didn't want to give it up. Jess had only been in London for two weeks, but already it felt like everything. What was she willing to give up to keep Jess in her life?

Eventually, Tabitha would catch them. Nothing good lasted forever. Marion knew she needed to get a new agent, one who respected her autonomy, but it would wait. She could worry about that in the future when she had a good reason to change things. For now, she would maintain the status quo.

Marion closed her eyes. She would steal as much of this time as the universe would allow her. She would wrap her arms around Jess and hold her close and one day maybe she would get to tell Jess everything that she was feeling, she would get to say something about the tightness in her chest that got harder to ignore every time Jess smiled at her.

I love you.

She wasn't ready to say it yet. Not while Tabitha might still find out and ruin her life. She felt as if saying the words aloud would bring everything crashing down around her ears. She would do her best to live in the moment and she would hold onto Jess as tightly as she could.

"You're sure you don't want to come to the concert tonight?" Jess lay sprawled across Marion's bed as she watched her pull clothes from the closet and toss them on the foot of the bed.

"In case you've forgotten, I have my own show tonight." She leaned down and placed a lingering kiss on Jess's lips.

"Call in sick. Let your understudy take it." Jess wrapped a hand around the base of Marion's skull and kept her close for another kiss. "Isn't that what understudies are for?"

"Jess, you know I can't." Marion crawled on top of Jess and kissed her again and again. "If I call in sick, Tabitha will be on the phone in five minutes with a lecture about professionalism."

Jess sighed. "I know. I just—I only have this night left before the tour starts again. I want to spend it with you."

"And you will. After the concert. I'll be here waiting." Marion levered herself up again. "Now, you need to get up and get dressed so you can go to the venue, and I need to get ready to go to the theater."

Jess grumbled. She was about to reach out for Marion again despite the demands of both of their schedules when the phone started to ring. Marion looked at Jess with wide eyes. There was only one person who would be calling her in London. Bile started to rise up in the back of her throat. The phone rang again. Marion lunged for it. She didn't want to think about the consequences of making Tabitha wait for her.

CHAPTER ELEVEN

Present Day

"So, what are your plans for today?" Jess asked as she looked up. She had just finished putting their dishes in the dishwasher after successfully making breakfast. Marion still wasn't entirely convinced that Jess could cook, but nothing had caught fire and the pancakes had been enjoyable enough.

"I have none." Marion shrugged loosely. Barring any need to re-record something, Marion was finished with the film. She had other projects lined up, but nothing that was starting soon.

Jess rounded the island to where Marion was sitting on a stool and slid her arms around Marion's neck as she leaned in for a kiss. Marion happily granted it.

"I wish I had time to get distracted by you, but Naomi is coming in this afternoon to record some of her songs, and unlike with you, I can't force her to stay for hours and hours." Jess kissed her again and then again.

"You should probably stop kissing me if you want to get there before noon." Marion nuzzled against Jess's neck and pulled her closer. Jess slid onto Marion's lap and kissed her again, more deeply this time. Marion splayed her hand over Jess's stomach and Jess's breath hitched.

"I don't want to stop kissing you." Jess scratched at the nape of Marion's neck. Marion shivered.

"If you keep doing that, we'll end up doing more than just kissing." Marion rubbed her hand over Jess's stomach and up toward her breasts.

"And if I want to do more than kiss you?" Jess husked into Marion's ear.

"You're the one who just said we don't have time." Marion cupped one of Jess's breasts and brushed her thumb over her nipple through her shirt and bra.

Jess tugged at Marion's hair and tilted her head back for another, more thorough kiss. They stayed like that for several long minutes just kissing as Marion continued to stroke Jess's nipple. She could feel it getting hard under her fingers. Jess sighed into Marion's mouth and gripped her shoulders. Finally, they pulled apart.

"If you don't get up, I won't be responsible for my actions." Marion moved her hand from Jess's breast to her thigh and swept it up to her hip.

"Fuck," Jess groaned and dropped her head onto Marion's shoulder. "If it were anyone other than Naomi, I'd say screw it and be late. Right now, I hate child labor laws."

Marion gently pushed Jess off of her lap. Standing, Jess straightened her skirt, pulling it back down as she took a step away and leaned against the counter. Marion took a deep breath and tried to center herself.

"My point was, if you're not doing anything later, you should come back over." Jess cupped both sides of Marion's face. "I'd like to see you again."

Marion turned her face into Jess's hand and placed a kiss against the center of her palm. "Are you sure that's wise?"

Jess laughed in good humor. "My life isn't so interesting as to inspire twenty-four-hour surveillance. Particularly not these past few years." She brushed some hair back from Marion's temple.

"This is interesting. Together, we're interesting." And Marion wasn't ready for her life to be splashed across TMZ's website or whoever specialized in celebrity gossip these days.

"Then it's a good thing nobody knows about this. And nobody is going to find out just because you come to dinner." Jess placed a light kiss on Marion's lips. "Please?"

Marion looked down at her hands. Jess was right. It was just dinner. Well, it was more than dinner, but it wasn't anything suspicious. There was no reason for anyone to pay attention to them.

"All right." Marion looked back up and leaned into the kiss Jess placed on her lips.

"Yay," Jess said. "I should be back by seven. You should take the extra key and just let yourself in if I'm not back by then."

Marion stared at Jess for a moment. "If that's what you want."

"It is. It's very much what I want." When Jess kissed her again, Marion had a feeling she was talking about more than just one night.

❖

Marion sat in her living room and tried to get absorbed into the script in her hands. It wasn't working. She wasn't sure if it was because the script wasn't worth her time, Margaret normally managed to weed those out, or if she was just distracted. She set the script aside and pinched the bridge of her nose. She could hear Barbara rattling around somewhere in the house, voice rising and falling as she talked on the phone with someone. She tried to focus on the half of that conversation she could hear, anything to take her mind off of Jess, but Barbara was simply too far away. She'd let Marion know if the conversation turned into something she needed to concern herself with, but until then, Marion would have to be content remaining in the dark.

The conversation wasn't really what was bothering her though. She took a deep breath and tried to center herself. It didn't work. Jess's smile from that morning when she agreed to come back for dinner, remained firmly planted in her mind. Nothing she did seemed to be able to banish it. Part of her wanted to revel in the feelings Jess stirred up, in the giddy energy that ran through her body. The other part of her trembled in fear. What did this mean? Things had seemed so easy that morning when she had kissed Jess good-bye. Now, all she could think of were what-ifs. What if someone had seen them together at the benefit the night before? What if someone noticed Marion going back for dinner later this evening? All it took was for one person to put everything together and suddenly her privacy would be gone, gone in an instant, sacrificed to the public's demand to know everything about her life. She knew she was being irrational, but she couldn't stop herself. The very thought of her face on the cover of a tabloid again filled her with dread.

Marion sighed deeply. She was getting ahead of herself. It was one dinner. There was every chance that she and Jess would find themselves to be wholly incompatible, that dinner would be awkward and uncomfortable, and they would never want to see each other again. An unsuccessful experiment in revisiting the past. Then she wouldn't have to worry about it anymore. Still, she hoped that wasn't the case. She wanted the ease she had felt with Jess in the past to reassert itself now. She longed for it.

She looked back at her script and picked it up. Staring at her hands would only make the day take even longer. A few more hours and she would be back at Jess's and she'd be too caught up to worry about these things. She just had to distract herself until that happened.

❖

"I brought Thai," Jess called out as she opened her front door and pushed it open with her body. Marion looked up from her spot on the couch. She put down her book and stood, meeting Jess in the kitchen and taking some of the food from Jess's overburdened arms and putting it down on the counter. "I wasn't sure what you liked, so I got an assortment."

"You know you could have called." Marion pulled containers out of paper bags and arranged them between them.

"I did think of that." Jess leaned in and placed a quick kiss on Marion's lips. "Then I realized I don't have your phone number. Just the one for your assistant. I figured you wouldn't appreciate me calling her to get your takeout order."

"That's easily fixed. And I'm sure I can find something to eat in all of this." Marion nodded toward the large expanse of food in front of them.

Jess pulled out her phone, unlocked it, and slid it across the counter to Marion. Marion picked it up and started to add in her contact information as Jess pulled out plates and opened containers. It was only after Marion finished and looked up that she realized Jess was staring at her.

"What?" Marion raised her eyebrows. "Is something wrong?"

"I just realized I missed a key step in saying hello to you." She sauntered around the island and toward Marion until she was close enough to wedge herself between Marion and the counter. She grabbed the collar of Marion's shirt with one hand and wrapped her other arm around Marion's neck, using both to pull Marion down and into a long kiss. Once it ended, she brushed her nose against Marion's cheek. "Hi."

Marion cleared her throat. "Hello." She pulled Jess in closer and reveled in the feeling of their bodies pressed together.

Jess cupped Marion's face and brushed her thumbs over Marion's cheeks. "I missed you."

The way Jess said it left Marion wondering if she was just talking about the afternoon or something more profound. If it was the latter, Marion wasn't sure exactly what she would do. After all, she had tried so hard to stop thinking about Jess, and she was sure Jess had done the same. Despite their past, they might as well be strangers now. It didn't feel like they were strangers. It already felt like they fit together too well, just like before.

How easy would it be to fall back into that? Marion could already feel the pull of Jess's curves, of her skin, of the smell of her hair when she first got out of the shower, and the taste of her lips right after she brushed her teeth. She could feel the pull of quiet dinners and long hours spent in Jess's bed. She felt herself getting carried away. Again.

"Stop thinking so hard." Jess kissed Marion again. "It's just dinner and maybe a movie, if you're agreeable. I hear you like those." She smiled up at Marion.

"I've been known to watch one on occasion," Marion said.

"Good. Now, let me open a bottle of wine and we can eat."

❖

1997

Marion looked up from her book as Jess used her key to open the door to Marion's flat. She didn't know when she'd started thinking of it as Jess's key, but the development made her happy. Maybe she'd let Jess keep it after she left, just in case she ended up in London again in the next few weeks.

Jess buzzed with energy as she practically skipped into the flat. Marion put her book aside and stood just in time to catch an exuberant Jess in her arms. "I take it things went well?" Jess's energy was catching, and Marion's face lit up.

"Spectacular. I'll be exhausted tomorrow, but right now I'm so fucking high I can't stand it. God, that's a rush. Why the hell do people take drugs when they can just do *that?*" Jess smashed their lips together, pulling Marion tight against her.

Marion laughed at how joyous Jess was. "Well, not all of us can do *that.*" Marion kissed her again as Jess's fingers found the buttons of her blouse.

"You're overdressed. I'm overdressed. We should be naked. We should be naked and in bed and together." Jess caught Marion's hands and dragged her toward the bedroom. Marion laughed and tripped after her.

It took seconds to get undressed, each shedding their clothes as quickly as possible. Jess seemed to shine with energy, reflecting it off of every surface. Marion grabbed Jess around the waist and pulled her close, kissing her as fiercely as she could.

"I feel amazing." Jess kissed Marion and pulled her down toward the bed. Once they were there, she pulled Marion on top of her. "I want to feel you inside me," she whispered as she nuzzled against Marion's cheek.

Marion groaned and arched against Jess, Jess's words sending a bolt through her. "Anything you want." Marion kissed Jess again. "Tonight, you get anything you want."

Jess trailed her fingers down Marion's spine as they lay in bed together. The sun was slowly creeping up the horizon and Marion wished more than anything that there was a way to stop time. She reached for Jess's other hand and laced their fingers together.

"I don't want this to end." Marion met Jess's eyes as she squeezed her hand. "I don't want you to leave."

Jess ran her fingers through Marion's hair. "I don't want to leave, but I don't have much choice. There are far too many people counting on me to make this tour successful. I can't just abandon it."

"I know. I would never ask that of you." Marion leaned in and placed a light kiss on Jess's lips. "I just wish there was a way." Marion shook her head. It was a daydream. A fantasy. They could never be together the way Marion wanted. They would forever be looking over their shoulders. Eventually, someone would figure it out. Still, if there *was* a way.

"Maybe if we just don't overthink it." Jess pulled Marion fully into her arms. "When do you wrap the play? It has to be soon, doesn't it?"

"Three weeks. Then I'm supposed to go back to Hollywood. My next film starts shooting in two months." Marion burrowed into Jess's arms.

"I'll be in Berlin in three weeks. Why don't you take some time and fly out? Stay with me for Berlin and Amsterdam. You can be back in Hollywood in plenty of time for your movie. And my tour will be over in a few months. We could see what happens." Jess shrugged.

"I—" Marion took a deep breath and seriously thought about it. They could pull this off for a while longer, couldn't they? Marion wanted it so badly. Jess had to leave in a few hours and Marion already ached with missing her. "Berlin?"

"And Amsterdam?" Jess brushed back some hair from Marion's face. "Say yes." Jess whispered. "Say yes."

Marion closed her eyes. She so rarely took risks. Everything in her life was planned for her. Tabitha had planned it all. Everything except for Jess. She couldn't have planned for Jess. She needed to say no. She needed to end this now. Someone would find out. Tabitha would find out. She opened her eyes again.

"Yes."

Chapter Twelve

Present Day

"I think we should throw a party."

Jess lifted her head from where it was resting against Marion's shoulder. They were sitting together on the couch. Jess had one of Marion's arms draped over her shoulders as Marion read and Jess worked on song lyrics. It had been a few weeks since they had rekindled their relationship and Marion had quickly gotten used to having Jess in her life once again. She had barely spent a night in her own bed in the last two weeks. Heaven knew what her assistant, Barbara, thought about her showing up at home close to ten every morning, obviously not having slept there. Barbara hadn't said anything about it, though.

"Why should we throw a party?" Marion asked drolly. Jess couldn't be serious. She had to know that Marion wasn't ready to announce their relationship to the world, and throwing a party together seemed like an excellent way to do just that.

"Because I'm happy. And I want other people to be happy. And I like parties." Jess looked up at Marion pleadingly.

Marion pursed her lips. "Then maybe *you* should throw a party."

Jess rolled her eyes. "Fine. I'll throw a party," she said, seeming to understand Marion's reluctance. "But you're coming, and you're helping me put together the guest list. I'm not going to have you being miserable surrounded by no one but my friends."

Jess flipped to a new sheet of paper in her notebook, pencil poised to start writing names down. "So, who am I inviting?"

Marion shook her head and kissed Jess's temple. "I'm not getting out of this, am I?"

"Nope." Jess bounced once in her seat, scooting even closer to Marion. "Names, please."

Marion closed her eyes and bowed to the inevitable.

Marion sipped her wine and looked around Jess's living room as the party flowed around her. Jess was holding court near the kitchen island, arms gesticulating as she told some sort of story to the cluster of people that surrounded her. The story was likely about something that had happened on one of her tours, and Marion was sure she'd get some version of it later if she even hinted at being curious. For now, she would give Jess her space. She preferred staying on the edges at these sorts of things. The party was small enough for her to keep track of most of the guests and Jess had managed the guest list with exquisite skill. It was a room full of actual friends and no one to impress, though really, Marion was past the point in her career that she needed to impress anyone to get a role.

Julia and her husband sat on the couch and made up another small grouping. Julia had given her and Jess a searching look when she had first arrived at the party, but she hadn't asked any questions that Marion would have been unwilling to answer, even to such an old friend.

Marion felt a presence at her side and when she angled herself in that direction, she found Lauren standing next to her.

"Something I can do for you?" Marion turned fully to look at Lauren.

"Not really. I just saw you and I thought I'd say hi." Lauren shrugged. "For a singer, Jess knows a lot of Hollywood people." She looked out over the guests. If she was trying to imply something, Marion couldn't tell. Maybe that was why Marion responded to the comment at all.

"I may have had some input into the guest list." Marion didn't look at Lauren as she said it, preferring to stare out the nearest window instead. It was as close as she was willing to come to acknowledging her relationship with Jess.

"Are you and Jess close? I didn't realize you were friends." Marion looked at Lauren, hunting for the innuendo that had to be hidden in that statement. She didn't find any.

How did she begin to explain what she and Jess were to each other without sharing too much? After their conversation in the parking lot of the studio, anything less than the full truth felt like a betrayal, but was she ready for that yet? Would Lauren understand how privileged that information would be? Surely, Lauren wouldn't run off to the papers, but it was unrealistic to expect her not to tell anyone at all, even just in passing. She was incredibly happy to be with Jess again, but she didn't want people speculating about her life.

Jess saved her from answering by breaking away from the people around her and walking toward them. As soon as she was close enough, Jess leaned up and brushed her lips over Marion's cheek. Marion blushed at the attention.

"I heard my name, and I saw you looking at me, and I thought I would come retrieve you from this corner where you're both hiding." Jess's smile sparkled as she looked between Marion and Lauren.

"I was just telling Marion how much I appreciated the invitation." Lauren looked down bashfully.

"Well, she insisted," Jess leaned in, "and I don't like telling Marion no." She tangled her fingers with Marion's and Marion allowed the contact for a moment before she squeezed Jess's hand and withdrew her own.

"I, um, yeah." Lauren looked flustered by the innuendo. "I can't imagine many people succeed in stopping you when you want something, do they?" She took a sip of her wine and looked between Jess and Marion.

Jess laughed and rubbed Marion's upper arm as Marion blushed and looked away. "I haven't any idea what you might be talking about."

"Of course, you don't, darling." Jess shook her head. "You really should come join the party though."

"I will in a bit." She knew Jess wouldn't let her hover on the edges all night and she would be required to interact with more people. For now, she was content with her conversation with Lauren, embarrassing as it might be.

"Good." Jess kissed Marion's cheek again before turning to Lauren. "Come find me when she's done holding you hostage. There's someone I want to introduce you to." She winked at Lauren then waved with her fingers before heading back to the center of the party.

"Is she always like that? You know, when she isn't working," Lauren asked as she watched Jess walk away.

"Like what?" Marion watched Jess too, but she quickly turned back to Lauren.

Lauren shrugged. "Happy, I guess. Sorta like a whirlwind."

Marion smiled softly and tried to hide her regret. "I am certain she isn't always happy, but yes, she is a bit of a whirling dervish no matter what mood she's in." Jess never had been very good at being still. "Now, tell me how you're doing. How are things with your parents?"

Lauren took a deep breath and looked down into her wine glass. "Things are—" She shook her head. "They're fine, I guess. Mom isn't talking to me. Dad says it's temporary and she'll get over it. I don't know." She took another sip of her wine. "This isn't the most festive topic of conversation."

"Of course." Marion smiled sympathetically. She saw how Lauren wouldn't find a party to be the best place to talk about such things. Still, she was worried about her. "You should come to dinner. Jess, for some unfathomable reason, actually likes to cook. She would enjoy having someone to show off for." Marion wasn't exactly sure why she extended the invitation. It was far too intimate, far too much of an invitation to see something she still wasn't comfortable showing to the world. But something about the pain Lauren was only barely concealing pushed her to it.

"Are you and Jess dating?" Lauren asked and Marion's eyes went wide. She hadn't expected such a blunt question, the one Lauren had been hinting at earlier but hadn't been able to ask. She wasn't ready to share the real answer. Her eyes rapidly found Jess and locked on her, as if she might be able to hear the conversation and come save her as she had earlier.

"Jess and I are perhaps more than friends." She tried to imbue her answer with the unspoken truth. She couldn't say more. Was *dating* even the correct way to define a relationship that happened primarily inside Jess's home? They hadn't gone on a proper date in more than twenty years.

"Ah. Right." Lauren nodded. She seemed to pick up on the unspoken nature of Marion and Jess's relationship. At least Marion hoped that she had. "Well, I'd be happy to be Jess's guinea pig, if that would make her happy."

"Good." Marion smiled a relieved smile. "I'll let you know the details once I've talked to Jess."

"Cool." Lauren smiled back at Marion and at the very least, she appeared not to be thinking about her parents.

"You should go mingle." Marion nodded toward the room.

"Right. Yeah. Thanks. For the invitation." Lauren ducked her head, pushed some hair behind her ear, and headed toward a group of other young actors she seemed to know.

Marion opened her eyes to moonlight streaming through the sheer curtains that covered Jess's windows. She still wasn't used to sleeping in a bed that wasn't her own. Jess was curled against her side, and Marion could feel her every exhale against her skin.

Even after twenty years had passed, Jess was still beautiful. Something in Latin over her ribs had joined the owl on her back. Splashes of color covered her wrists and arms, hips and thighs, and Marion had spent at least an hour looking at each one, coaxing the stories behind them out of Jess, even the ones she'd only gotten on a whim. She couldn't stop looking at the violets, wanting to run her fingers over them, and thinking about what they might mean, why Jess might have gotten them. But she wouldn't wake Jess with the touch or her questions.

Marion nuzzled against the top of her head and placed a kiss there. Jess shifted beside her but didn't wake. Marion knew if she tried to roll out of bed that would change. How worried was Jess that Marion might disappear again? And why was she willing to take that risk? Even knowing her own motivations, Marion didn't know if she could be as brave.

Marion rolled toward Jess and pulled her into her arms. What was she willing to do to keep this? To keep something that already seemed more serious than was probably warranted? What was she willing to compromise?

❖

1997

Marion smiled as she pushed open the door to her dressing room. They had only five performances left, just one week, and she was already thinking about afterward. She had booked her flight to Berlin earlier in the day and she couldn't wait to see Jess again. She didn't know what would happen after that, but she didn't care. Whatever happened would be worth it. It was much, much too soon, but her feelings for Jess overwhelmed her. So caught up in her plans for the future, it took Marion more than a few seconds to realize she wasn't alone.

Marion stopped short. "Tabitha." Her agent. What was her agent doing in her dressing room? What was she even doing in London? The last Marion had heard, she was in Hollywood.

"Marion." Tabitha's voice was hard as she stood from where she had been sitting in Marion's chair. She stepped aside and motioned for Marion to take a seat. Marion's stomach churned, but she did as she was bid.

"What are you doing here?" Marion tried to keep a pleasant tone. There was no reason for her to feel such trepidation. There were myriad reasons for Tabitha to be in her dressing room. Still, nothing good came to mind.

"Since when have you started making friends with pop stars," Tabitha sneered.

Marion licked her lips. "I don't know what you mean." Jess. This was about Jess. How much did Tabitha know? How did she know anything?

"Don't lie to me, girl." Tabitha put her hands on Marion's shoulders, her nails digging in a bit too sharply. "Jessica Carmichael," she spit out. "I knew I couldn't trust you to spend six months in London on your own without my supervision. It's a good thing I had someone watching you for me."

"I don't—" Marion looked up at Tabitha through the mirror. Maybe there was a way to salvage this. She swallowed nervously. "Why is that a problem? She's just a friend." There was no way Tabitha could know about anything else, was there? Marion tried to think back to every moment she and Jess had spent together in public, but it was impossible.

"Is she? Is she *just a friend*?" Tabitha narrowed her eyes. "Dyke."

Marion flinched. Tabitha had never been a pleasant person, but Marion had never heard such venom in her voice. Her eyes went wide.

"Did you enjoy fucking her?" Tabitha tightened her grip on Marion's shoulders. "I hope you did because you won't get another opportunity." She shoved Marion forward, forcing Marion to catch herself against the vanity. Her wrists protested. Marion couldn't breathe. This was exactly what she had been afraid of. It was over. Everything was over.

"I should quit. I should walk away from you and your perversions." Tabitha crossed her arms. "It's fortunate for you that I like you, Marion." She smiled but her eyes remained hard. "And I'm not going to go to the press with this."

Marion tried to swallow. She gripped the vanity harder. Her knuckles turned white. "I…I don't…I…"

"We are going to fix this. We are going to pretend it never happened. You will *never* see Jessica Carmichael again. If you do, you will make it abundantly clear that this past month was a mistake and that you are *not like her.* If she wants to throw away a perfectly good career that is not *our* problem."

"But—" Marion pleaded.

"Anything else and I will tell the *Sun*, the *Mail*, and the *Mirror* that Jessica Carmichael is a lesbian and she will be finished."

"I'll fire you. I will." Marion tried to stand up for herself. It was the hardest thing she had ever done, harder even, than saying good-bye to her parents when they had gone back to London and left her in Tabitha's care. Marion couldn't remember a time in her life when Tabitha hadn't been her agent, hadn't been hovering at the edges of her life, controlling her every move, every film, every interview, every appearance, everything. Tabitha, she was a constant. Marion's only constant. After her parents had left, Marion hadn't had anyone else.

She had been there in the past, when Marion was a teenager, when she'd barely known what a lesbian was, let alone thought of herself as one. Tabitha had threatened her then and told her to stay away from the girls she had lingered over on set.

As she had gotten older, the threat had seemed less important than the few women she found to spend the night with here or there. Sneaking around had been a thrill, but it hadn't prepared her for Jess. Jess, who was only supposed to be another one-night affair.

But Jess was more than that now. Jess was everything. Marion didn't know what her life would look like without Tabitha in it, but she would try. For Jess, she would try.

"No, you won't, girl. All of your success, you owe that to me. If you fire me, it all goes away. The films, the awards, everything. I tell the entire world about you and you never work again. And Jess, well, let's see how supportive those mothers and fathers of teenage girls really are, shall we?"

Marion's face crumpled. If Tabitha had threatened only her, maybe she could have withstood it, maybe she would have been brave enough, but she couldn't let Tabitha ruin Jess. She couldn't. Marion dropped her head into her hands and pressed her palms against her eyes.

"Do you understand, Marion? One word and it's over."

Marion swallowed against the lump in her throat. "I understand." Marion wouldn't cry. She refused to cry. She refused to give Tabitha the satisfaction.

"Good girl." Tabitha turned to leave. "Now, get dressed. We're going to dinner with a producer I want you to charm."

CHAPTER THIRTEEN

Present Day

"And that's what happens when you let an overly energetic boxer puppy onto a tour bus." Jess smiled as Lauren and Marion laughed at the anecdote. They had passed a pleasant dinner together, mainly thanks to Jess and her endless stories about touring across the world. If Lauren realized they hadn't touched on Jess's first tour at all, she didn't mention it. In fact, Lauren had been unfailingly polite the entire night. Marion wondered if there was a way to get her to relax a bit. She wanted to make sure Lauren was doing well, but she didn't want it to seem like she was interrogating her.

"So, did you guys meet working on *Petunia's Potion*?" Lauren looked between them. "It just doesn't seem like you've only known each other a couple of months."

Marion looked at Jess trying to figure out how she would want her to respond. Jess looked just as torn as Marion was feeling. Finally, Marion needed to say something. "We met at a party in the late nineties but we…fell out of touch." It was the most tactful way Marion could think to phrase it. "The film has given us a chance to get reacquainted."

Jess reached out for Marion's hand on the tabletop, and Marion allowed her to take it. "I'm incredibly glad that it did." Marion looked down at their joined hands. Her first instinct was to pull away, but after a glance at Lauren, and seeing no judgment on her face, she left her hand where it was.

Just as Marion was starting to get comfortable, Jess stood and grabbed her wine glass. "Come on, I'm going to curl up on the couch. You two should come with me. Bring the wine." She tugged on Marion's hand and without thinking about it, Marion followed her. As soon as she sat down on the couch, Jess did exactly as she said she would and curled herself against Marion, manhandling her into place and draping Marion's arm over her shoulders as she lounged against her. Lauren, left with the bottle of wine, topped up their glasses and sat in a low-slung leather club chair.

"Take off your heels. Get comfortable. I'll make drinks." Jess said to Lauren. Lauren's eyes went wide, and she looked between Marion and Jess.

"You absolutely do not have to keep drinking if you don't want to." Marion wanted to make sure Lauren knew that her continued presence wasn't conditioned on her drinking too much.

Lauren opened her mouth, then hesitated, as if looking for the right thing to say. It looked like she finally made up her mind. "Well, I don't think this glass of wine is going to last much longer." A mischievous smile tugged at her lips as she took a sip of the mentioned wine.

"Of course not." Jess rolled her eyes. "I'm having vodka." She uncurled herself despite just having gotten comfortable. "Yes, I know, darling," Jess kissed the top of Marion's head. "You want scotch. What's your drink of choice?" She directed her question at Lauren.

"Um." Lauren looked between them. "Bourbon? If you have it."

"I absolutely have bourbon. Ice?" Jess headed back into the kitchen.

"Just a bit of water."

Jess got glasses, a bottle of water from the fridge, pulled the vodka out of the freezer, and deposited all of it on the coffee table before going over to the bar and grabbing two bottles. Soon, she had reclaimed her seat under Marion's arm.

"There. Now we're set." She poured herself a drink. Neither Marion nor Lauren moved.

"Well, don't wait for me." Jess shook her head in amusement. Marion sighed and reached around Jess for the bottle of scotch. A minute later and she had two fingers sitting in a cut crystal tumbler. Lauren was right behind her.

❖

"My parents suck. I mean, they could suck worse. They didn't disown me or anything. And even if they did, it isn't like I can't survive on my own. But I really didn't think they would act like this." Lauren snuggled down farther into the chair and wrapped a blanket around her shoulders. Marion wasn't exactly sure where she had gotten the blanket from, but she was glad Lauren had something to provide her with some sort of comfort.

"Come here." Before Marion could react, Jess was out of her arms and around the coffee table, holding her arms out to Lauren. Lauren seemed to sigh in relief as she stood up and let herself fall into Jess's arms. The two clung to each other for what felt like ages before Jess rubbed Lauren's back and let her go.

"I'm sorry your parents suck." Jess resettled on the couch.

Lauren shrugged and looked down into her glass. "Maybe they'll come around."

Marion was skeptical, but she only had her own uncaring parents and Tabitha as a reference point, so she admitted to a bit of bias. "If they don't," Marion swallowed, "we're here to support you." She wasn't sure what made her say it, maybe it was the scotch, but she found she meant it. If Lauren needed something, she felt comfortable enough to offer both her and Jess's help.

Lauren looked up in surprise. "I…you really don't have to."

Marion waved her off. "I know I don't have to, but I am more than old enough to do only the things I want to do. Do you understand?"

"Yeah. Thank you."

Marion reached over and poured Lauren another drink.

❖

"I want to write a screenplay." Lauren's head lolled back on the back of the chair. "I'm *writing* a screenplay. It's almost done. I mean, I don't think I could do it full time. I like acting. I love acting. I just have these ideas, y'know? And I have to get them out. It probably isn't any good." She kept staring at the ceiling.

Marion looked at her too intently for the amount she'd had to drink. Her head swam and it was hard to focus, but she knew the kind of uncertainty Lauren was feeling. She'd spent most of her early career feeling exactly the same way, though she'd been a teenager at the time. "If you want to write a screenplay, then write it. It doesn't matter if it's terrible if you find working on it fulfilling."

Lauren sighed. "I know that. I do. And most of the time, that's enough. But I really, really want to see it produced. And no one is going to do that if it sucks."

"Send it to me." Marion tightened her hold on Jess, who was half asleep and only vaguely listening to them. "If it's terrible, I'll tell you. If it's good, I'll find you a production company. Or I'll produce it myself." Marion shrugged as if it really was that simple. "Don't," she held up a finger, "say I don't have to do it."

Lauren shut her mouth, but it only lasted for a second. "Okay."

"Good." Marion nodded. "Now, I think it's time to pour you into the guest bed. There's no chance I'm putting you in an Uber tonight." She jostled Jess enough to wake her up and at her questioning noise, whispered, "Bed," before kissing her temple and forcing her upright. Even though she was unsteady on her feet. Marion shooed both of them up the stairs. Jess disappeared into her bedroom while Marion took Lauren down the hall. She opened the guest room door for Lauren.

Lauren steadied herself on the doorjamb. "You and Jess are really cool. Like, really cool. It's awesome that you guys found each other and that you're happy together."

Marion could only shake her head. "Give me a minute and I'll find something for you to sleep in."

Lauren nodded and stepped into the room. "Cool."

Marion walked back down the hallway to Jess's room. Jess was nowhere to be found, likely in the bathroom, but Marion knew where she kept an old T-shirt or two and quickly grabbed one before heading back to the guest room. Lauren was already asleep on top of the covers, so Marion just left the shirt on the foot of the bed before leaving the room and gently closing the door behind her.

Jess was sitting on the edge of the bed rubbing lotion into her hands when Marion returned to Jess's bedroom.

"You're very sweet with her, you know." Jess nodded in the general direction of the guest room.

Marion blushed. She shook her head and then started removing her jewelry. "She clearly needs someone to look out for her."

"Mm-hmm." Jess got up and wrapped her arms around Marion from behind.

Marion sighed. "I just wish I had had someone when I was her age. Maybe I could have been braver. Maybe things would have been different." Marion closed her eyes and sank into Jess's arms. Jess pressed a kiss to one of Marion's shoulder blades.

"How can you do this? How can you trust me again?" It had been bothering Marion, but she hadn't been brave enough to ask until now. The scotch made it easier.

Jess kissed Marion's shoulder blade again. "I don't...it was that night we all went for drinks. The conversation we had in the car. It made me realize that maybe everything that happened wasn't about me. I didn't think about how scared you must have been. And we were so young then. It's easy to take memories and put more weight on them than they held at the time. Yes, you hurt me, but you've apologized, and I'm willing to put the past behind us."

Marion dropped her head to her chest and took a deep breath. "I don't know that I'm worth it. I don't know that I'm worthy of your forgiveness. Or this second chance."

Jess tightened her arms around Marion. "Well, then it's a good thing it's my decision and not yours. Now, get undressed and come to bed. It's late, or early, but either way, it's time to go to sleep now."

Marion nodded and Jess let her go. "I'll be there in a minute." She turned and placed a gentle kiss on Jess's lips before she headed toward the bathroom.

❖

Marion heard the guest bedroom door open and close across the hallway. Jess had left the door cracked when she had gotten up, one of the rare mornings when she had awoken before Marion. Marion listened to the sound of Lauren's feet as she headed toward the living room. She could hear Jess lightly singing to herself, nonsense syllables that might or might not turn into a fully realized song one day. The singing stopped and Marion could only imagine it was because Lauren had stepped into the room.

She heard murmured good mornings and the sound of a mug being placed on the counter. Jess would have offered Lauren coffee; she'd probably need it after how much they'd had to drink the night before.

"Did you sleep okay?" Jess asked.

"Yeah. It was fine. Better than I expected." Marion could practically hear Lauren yawning. "Excuse me."

Marion supposed she should get up and join them, but the bed was still warm, and it smelled like Jess.

"She was different last night," Lauren said and now Marion knew she should get up. If they were going to talk about her, she should let them know she was listening.

"She's very private." That was Jess.

"Yeah. I figured that out. I wouldn't…I'm not…I appreciate your trust. Her trust."

"Good. She doesn't open up to many people." Marion heard Jess moving around.

"Yeah." Lauren paused again. "I wanted to say good-bye, but I should probably be going."

"Of course, I'll see you out." The sound of feet padded farther away, then the front door opened and closed. Then the feet got closer until the door to the bedroom opened. Jess walked in and crawled back onto the bed.

"How much of that did you hear?" Jess snuggled into Marion's side on top of the covers. Marion turned into it and wrapped an arm around Jess's waist.

"Hmm…all of it." She accepted the kiss Jess placed on her lips.

"You didn't want to come out and say good-bye?"

"I'll call her later." Marion found Jess's lips again. "Right now, I'm more interested in you." She slid her hand under the hem of Jess's shirt.

Jess laughed joyfully. "How aren't you hung over?"

"Just luck." Marion slid her hand even farther under Jess's shirt and unhooked her bra. A minute later, Jess was topless and Lauren was far from either of their minds.

❖

Marion cocked her head to the side as she felt the vibration of her phone in her purse. She was sitting at a café eating lunch, and she was tempted not to answer it. Still, she was waiting for Barbara to tell her whether or not the latest draft of the screenplay Lauren wrote had arrived. It had been over a month since she and Jess had hosted Lauren for dinner and Lauren had sent her a draft of her screenplay *Hallowed Hills* the next day. Marion had been impressed. It wasn't perfect, but it was a solid first effort and it would make an excellent film. With a little help and the backing of the production company Marion had started when she got involved in *Petunia's Potion*, it hadn't taken long to attach a director to the project. She'd briefly thought about telling the director she needed to pick someone else for the lead role, but in the end, she had been too selfish. She was supposed to have received the completed script the week before, but rewrites had delayed it.

So, she pulled her phone out and looked down at the screen, but instead of Barbara, she saw Jess's name. She smiled as she answered it.

"Hello."

"Hi, you." Something inside Marion relaxed just hearing Jess's voice.

"What can I do for you?" Marion leaned back into her seat.

"Come join me for lunch." Jess's voice was light.

"I'm already at lunch. My food will be here soon." Marion shook her head even though Jess couldn't see her. If Jess had called ten minutes earlier Marion would have joined her in a heartbeat. She just wanted to be near Jess and she'd take any excuse to do it.

"Then tell me where you are and I'll come to you."

Marion laughed. "I'll be finished by the time you get here."

"I don't care. Do you care?" Marion could hear the way Jess was smiling.

"I'm on the patio at Basil." Marion gave in, shaking her head as she did it. She couldn't believe Jess would drive so far out of her way just to have lunch with her when there were so many more convenient options near the studio.

"I'll be there in twenty minutes."

"You'll be here in half an hour." Marion rolled her eyes. Even half an hour was ambitious, but Marion would wait for her anyway.

"Give me twenty minutes and then order me some spring rolls."

Marion chuckled, but she would do what Jess wanted her to do. She was pretty sure she would always do what Jess wanted her to do.

Jess flung herself into the chair across from Marion and smiled at the spring rolls waiting for her. "You're a dream." Her smile grew as she looked at Marion. "I wish I could kiss you silly right now."

Marion couldn't stop the blush that heated her cheeks. "The sentiment is mutual." She hoped no one was listening to them. The entire town might think that she was gay, but she had no desire to confirm or flaunt it. She didn't want their attention, she wanted Jess. But there was no subtlety in dating Jess. Were they even dating? Marion didn't want to ask.

Jess practically inhaled the first of the spring rolls before the server came over and took her order then poured her a glass of wine. As soon as the server was finished, Jess lounged back in her seat and pulled off her sunglasses.

"So, what have you been up to all morning?" Jess pressed her ankle against Marion's and Marion pressed back.

Then Marion frowned.

"Oh, that doesn't look promising." Jess grinned at her.

Marion couldn't help herself. She laughed. She was sure she had smiled more in the last few months than she had in the entire year before. "I'm supposed to be reviewing Lauren's script for *Hallowed Hills*, but she keeps doing rewrites. I'll be surprised if it's even the same movie by the time she's finished it."

"Will it really change that much?" Jess sipped her wine.

"It had better not. It was good enough the first time around." Marion was annoyed enough by the rewrites as it was. Marion sighed. "But she and the director are both young. I should have known better before I said yes, but they've got a promising vision, and even I can be blinded by hope."

"Is that so?" Jess teased her. "God, I just…" She looked at Marion with bright eyes. "It's too bad we're too level-headed now for assignations in bathrooms. I want to drag you off and spend the rest of the afternoon, and well, I think you can fill in the blank."

Marion looked down at her hands as she blushed once more. She could still remember that evening. They had been so reckless, so caught up in each other.

"Glad I'm not the only one who remembers that." Jess laughed again.

"I remember all of it." She remembered those few days in Hollywood and the entire month they had been together in London, how very happy she had been and then everything that came after.

Jess looked like she had been poleaxed. "You…" She swallowed, looked down and then looked back up. "You do?"

Marion met her eyes but could only nod. Her mouth was dry.

"I do too." Jess reached across the table and took Marion's hand. Marion flipped her palm up where they could hold each other's hands. Jess squeezed her hand tightly. Marion squeezed back. They were still like that when the server returned and placed Jess's order in front of her.

Jess thanked the woman and finally let go of Marion's hand. She cleared her throat. "So, I'm doing a benefit concert at the Hollywood Bowl in a few weeks."

"Yes, I've seen your face on a billboard or ten." Marion smirked and tried to get them back to the lighter atmosphere of the beginning of their lunch.

Jess rolled her eyes. "I'm trying to invite you, but you're making it very hard. Unless my music has devolved from *not terrible* to deplorable?"

"Your music is adequate, I suppose." Marion tried not to think of the collection of Jess's albums that sat on her bookshelf at home. Listening to Jess was an indulgence she had allowed herself only when she was feeling particularly masochistic, but she had listened. And still did.

Like that, Jess laughed again. "An improvement then. Tell me you'll come. Suffer through one concert, and I'll never make you come to another."

Marion didn't know why she was hesitating. It should have been easy to say yes. She sighed in acquiescence. "It's going to be excessively loud, isn't it?"

"We'll get you ear plugs. We'll find you a place backstage. It isn't as loud back there." Jess's eyes sparkled.

"I suppose that would be acceptable." Marion sipped her wine. It would be fine. She would be backstage. If she was nervous, it wasn't about attending the concert, it was about what would happen afterward, what was happening with her and Jess. Jess wouldn't be content with stolen lunches forever. What would happen when she asked for more? Would Marion be able to give it to her? She didn't need an answer just then, but she *would* need one, and soon.

❖

1997

Marion gripped her watch in her hand. She didn't need to look at it to know what time it was. She was supposed to be getting on a flight. She was supposed to be that much closer to Jess. A few hours from now, Jess would be at the airport waiting for her. She would never show up.

She sat on her couch in her empty flat, surrounded by luggage bound for Hollywood. If she turned her head just right, she would swear she could still smell Jess's perfume. She wished she had one of Jess's shirts, something that belonged to her to remember her by. She told herself she was being silly. They had barely had a month together in London. She shouldn't be this attached. It was ridiculous. No one fell in love in a month. And Jess couldn't possibly return her feelings, not as strongly. It was delusional to think that Jess felt that way about her. She wasn't worth it. This would just save Jess the trouble of leaving later.

Marion drew her knees up in front of herself and wrapped her arms around them. She swallowed around the tightness in her throat. She looked at her watch again. The airplane would be taking off soon. She wouldn't be on it.

She squeezed her watch even tighter until the edges bit into her skin. There would be marks there in the morning, reminders of her loss. She would rub the fingers of her other hand over them and remember why they were there. She was a coward. She was a coward and the marks would remind her of that. It was an impossible choice, and she had made the wrong one. She'd made the only one she could. Telling herself that didn't bring her any comfort.

With a last look at her watch, Marion tossed it aside. She buried her face in her knees, and finally, she cried.

Chapter Fourteen

Present Day

Marion fingered the backstage pass before she slipped it over her head and settled it over her chest. Her driver opened the car door and she nodded to him. She would be getting a ride with Jess when everything was finished, so she tipped him and sent him on his way. Her black jeans were tighter than she preferred, but Barbara had assured her they looked good on her and what else exactly did one wear to a pop concert?

A security guard carefully examined her pass then waved her through the door. Once she was inside, she wasn't sure what to do with herself. Jess had instructed her to come by her dressing room, but Marion didn't have the first idea about how to find it.

Just as she was about to ask someone, a voice called to her out of the stream of people flowing around her.

"Ms. Hargreaves." The young man came to a stop in front of her. "Jess sent me to take you back to her."

"Did she?" Marion pursed her lips. The boy radiated energy that Marion didn't share.

"Yep. It's just this way, ma'am." He started down a side hallway.

"And who, exactly, are you?" She might as well make small talk with him. It seemed like it was going to be quite a walk.

"I'm Tommy. Thomas." He blinked. "Anyway, I'm an intern."

"An intern?" No wonder he looked so young.

"Yes, ma'am." Tommy reached a door with a conspicuous star on it. He rapped hard on it twice before swinging it open. "If you wait here, Jess will be back from makeup soon."

"Thank you, Tommy." Marion nodded at him.

"No worries." He smiled at her before he disappeared back down the hallway, jogging off to do whatever he had to do now that he wasn't playing tour guide to a wayward actress who felt entirely out of place.

Marion looked around the room. It didn't look much different from any of the hundreds of dressing rooms she had used over the years, though there were substantially more sequins.

She took a seat in a side chair and tried to get comfortable while she waited.

Her mind was just starting to wander when the door opened and Jess strode through.

"Marion!" Jess didn't wait for Marion to stand. She simply straddled her lap and pulled her into a kiss. Between Jess's work in the studio, rehearsals for the concert, and the exhaustion that came with doing both at the same time, Jess and Marion hadn't seen each other in more than a week. It was good to know Jess had missed her, but she hadn't anticipated this level of enthusiasm. Her hands went to Jess's hips to hold her steady while they kissed.

Jess sighed happily as the kiss ended, and she sat back on Marion's lap. She brushed her thumb over Marion's lips to remove the smudges of her too bright lipstick.

"You came." Jess closed her eyes for a moment of quiet contentment.

"I did." Marion looked up at Jess.

"I'm so glad." Jess ran her fingers through Marion's loose hair.

Marion smiled up at her. "I wouldn't be anywhere else." She had felt completely out of place in the hallway, but here in Jess's dressing room she felt calm again.

"As much as I would love to stay here and make out with you the rest of the night, I suspect the seventeen thousand people sitting outside wouldn't be happy with me." Jess kissed her one last time before she got up off of Marion's lap. "Did you meet Tommy?"

"The child who showed me back here?" Marion pursed her lips.

"Yes, him." Jess laughed. "You're going to have to spend a little more time with him. He's going to show you a good place to see everything from backstage."

"Does he have any sort of job other than to babysit me for the night?"

"Not really." Jess looked at her impishly. "I promise, he normally does highly educational things. He's just been seconded to you for the night. If you need anything, he's at your disposal."

"I'm sure I'll be fine. I'm not the one entertaining those seventeen thousand people." Marion watched as Jess touched up her lipstick.

"Well, I need to get dressed, so you need to disappear, or I'll get completely distracted." Jess held her hand out to

Marion which she took as she stood. "I'll see you afterward?" Jess stepped close to Marion and looked up at her.

"I'll be wherever Tommy puts me," Marion replied before Jess kissed her one last time and pushed her out of the room.

❖

Marion watched as Jess jogged back off stage following her second encore. Marion could hear the roar of the crowd from where she was standing. She had been able to hear it all night. She thought she might be feeling just a fraction of what Jess felt while she performed. It was exhilarating. It was like being on stage at a theater only a thousand times more intense, a thousand times bigger.

What would it feel like if she could get on stage before that many people? She had always shied away from such large-scale theater events. Maybe she would have Margaret look into it if she was presented the opportunity again. They staged Shakespeare at the Hollywood Bowl sometimes, and there was always the summer series in Central Park.

She didn't have time to think about it anymore as a pink blur caught her attention, and before she could react, Jess threw her arms around Marion's neck and pulled her down to kiss her.

Before their lips could meet, Marion turned tense in Jess's arms and pulled back.

"What…?" Jess looked at Marion in confusion. "What's wrong?"

Marion swept her eyes over all of the people rushing around them. Between the stagehands, the dancers, the technicians, the musicians, and the interns, it felt like a thousand people were staring at them. Marion's spine went rigid.

"Marion." Jess reached down and took Marion's hand. "No one here cares." Marion didn't grasp Jess's hand back. "If they cared, they wouldn't be working for me. Everyone in the world knows that I'm bi."

Marion took half a step back. "That may be, but no one knows I'm a lesbian."

Jess looked at Marion in confusion. "Marion, darling," Marion flinched at the term of endearment. Jess wasn't keeping her voice down. Anyone could hear. "If you wanted that rumor quashed, you should have done something about it years ago. Everyone in town knows..." Jess shook her head in confusion.

"Everyone in town thinks they know. It isn't the same thing as knowing, and I have every intention of keeping it that way. And until this moment, no one knew about us." Marion took another step away.

Jess blinked. "That's the real problem, isn't it?" She swallowed as she looked up at Marion. "You're fine with this as long as no one knows you're sleeping with the pop star."

"I just don't want my life to be fodder for the tabloids," Marion shot back.

"What did you think would happen when we started this? Did you think we could keep it quiet indefinitely? Is that what you wanted?" Jess balled her hands into fists. "Because if that's what you wanted, you never should have come to this concert."

"Jess..." Marion couldn't believe they were doing this now. She couldn't believe they were doing it at all. She had thought...she didn't know what she had thought.

Jess shook her head. "No, Marion, I can't be with someone who wants to keep me a secret. I've done that before. We've done that before. I'm not doing it again."

"I'm sorry, but I can't live my life in front of everyone in the world."

"Well, I do live parts of my life in front of everyone in the world, and you knew that before you took me to bed." Jess shook her head. Before Marion could respond, Jess took her hand and pulled her through the corridors and back to her dressing room. She let Marion's hand go and paced to the other side of the room.

"I'm not asking you to appear on the cover of *Time* magazine or cry to Oprah. There aren't any cameras back here. There aren't any journalists. Kissing me isn't a grand statement." Jess huffed.

"Be that as it may, my life isn't for public consumption. I don't tweet. I don't post pictures to Instagram or do whatever one does with Snapchat. I work and sometimes I go out to a benefit dinner where no one really cares who I am as long as I'm giving them money. I get dressed up three times a year and have my picture taken and submit myself to impersonal interviews about my dress and my jewelry. That is the extent of my public life and I don't want that to change." Marion crossed her arms.

"Everything changes. Can't you see that? We can keep this quiet, but we can't keep it a secret forever. I won't be your secret. I do tweet and I do post pictures to Instagram and no one over the age of twenty-five understands Snapchat." Jess tried to inject some levity into the situation.

Marion didn't laugh.

"Why did you come here tonight?" Jess looked at Marion seriously.

"Because you asked me to. I didn't come to make some sort of semi-public statement."

"Fine. That's…that's fine." Jess rubbed her forehead. "Look, I know we aren't talking about the past, about what happened, but I need to know that it isn't going to happen again. I need to know that you're taking this seriously. I thought that's what tonight meant, that you might not be comfortable in front of the whole world, but that at least you'd be comfortable here. I wanted…I wanted to come off that stage and throw myself into your arms and have you catch me."

"Jess." Marion crossed the room and hesitantly reached out for Jess. "I do." She swallowed against the dryness in her throat. "I do take this seriously."

Jess took a deep breath and closed her eyes against the tears welling up in them. "But that's just it. I don't know if words are enough anymore. I want to be able to hold your hand while we walk down the street. I want to be able to come with you to those benefit dinners and awards shows and have you come with me to mine. I can't, I can't have anything less than that. And I don't want to wait for some unknown date when you'll be ready because it sounds to me like you'll never be ready." Jess stepped away from Marion and shook her head.

"I'm sorry. I don't think I can do this. Not if you want to keep hiding." Jess bit her lip as she looked at Marion expectantly. "Is that what you want?"

Jess held her breath. Marion knew what she wanted to hear. She knew. She knew what Jess wanted. But she couldn't. She wasn't ready, not for that, not for her face to be all over Jess's Instagram feed or on the cover of a tabloid.

She couldn't tell Jess what she wanted to hear.

Jess held up a hand as the threatened tears started to fall. "I need you to leave."

"Jess…" Marion reached out again only to have Jess avoid her touch.

"Just go." Jess crossed her arms over her stomach.

Marion took a deep breath, felt tears coming to her eyes as well.

"All right. I'll go." It wasn't what Marion wanted to say, but she didn't know what else she could do. She turned toward the door and let herself out.

❖

1997

Marion sat at the outdoor bar and sipped at her scotch. The heat pressed down on her until she felt like she couldn't breathe, couldn't move. She was stuck in place. Her *date* for the night was inside talking to a director who wasn't going to give him the time of day, but he had ignored her when she had told him as much. It had been seventy-four days since she had last seen Jess and she still thought about her every day. Tabitha's imposed dates only made the situation worse. Each one only made her wish that she was with Jess even more. She hoped that they would stop when her filming schedule started to pick back up again the next week.

Marion took a deep breath and held her scotch glass to her temple even though it wasn't cold enough to do any good. She just wanted the night to be over.

"I should have known you'd be here." It was more a whisper than actual spoken words.

Marion's breath caught in her chest and her heart stuttered. She turned too quickly to find Jess standing at the bar next to her.

"Jess," she exhaled as if seeing a ghost. She honestly thought she would never see Jess again. Now that Jess was beside her, she didn't know what to do. She wanted to tell her, to pull her aside and apologize and beg Jess to forgive her. She wanted so much. A wave from her date across the room brought Tabitha's threat back to the forefront of her mind. Did he know? Was he feeding Tabitha information? There was no way for her to know. She couldn't risk it.

"Marion." Jess's voice was small and tentative. She looked like she wanted to reach out but was only just keeping the desire at bay. Her champagne flute trembled.

"You should take your *blanc de blanc* and leave." Marion turned away from Jess. She couldn't show any interest. The shorter the conversation, the better.

"What happened? Berlin—you didn't show up. I waited at the airport for hours." Jess shook her head.

"Some of us have careers. Serious ones that don't allow us to flit off to other countries on a whim." Marion looked back at the mirror behind the bar. She couldn't look at Jess directly any longer.

"How can you? I thought…what we had…" Jess looked at Marion in confusion, and Marion wanted to reach out and smooth away the lines on her forehead. She wanted so badly to tell Jess the truth. She couldn't.

"We didn't have anything. We had a fling." Marion tried to be as dismissive, as disaffected as possible.

"That wasn't a fling. It was something more." Jess reached out for Marion's arm, but Marion shrugged her hand off as soon as she made contact.

"Maybe for you, but I'm not like you." Marion shook her head condescendingly. "It was just a poorly-thought-out experiment."

"You don't believe that. You *can't* believe that." Jess pleaded. Marion could see the tears gathering in her eyes as she slowly accepted the truth. God, Marion wanted to stop, but she needed to keep going.

"Go away. This conversation is over." She tossed back the rest of her scotch and stood.

As she walked past, Jess caught Marion's arm. "It isn't. It can't be. Marion, I was...I was falling in love with you."

"It was one month, Jess. You were falling in love with a dream. It was never going to be anything else. If you can't understand that, then you should keep your distance." Marion had fallen in love with that dream. She wanted it back. She couldn't have it. All she could do was protect Jess, keep Jess away from her, keep Jess safe.

Marion walked away without looking back until she reached her date. If Jess had any hope left, Marion needed to quash it. It was nothing to pull him down into a slightly less than discreet kiss. His stubble scratched at her, but she reminded herself that it wasn't real. The way his lips pressed against hers was nothing like the way it felt when Jess kissed her. It was all she could do to end the kiss with grace. She looked over at Jess as it ended and watched her face fall. It was for the best. Jess needed to know Marion was telling the truth.

Marion took hold of her date's arm and forced herself to press close to him. There were people at the party she needed to talk to. She hated networking. She would do it anyway. It was hardly the worst thing she would do that night.

Chapter Fifteen

Present Day

Marion pulled into the parking lot at the recording studio, automatically checking the lot for Jess's car. It wasn't there, and Marion didn't know whether to be relieved that she wouldn't run into her that day, or sad for the same reason. They hadn't seen each other since they had broken up. Marion supposed that was normal. They had avoided seeing each other for years. A few weeks wouldn't be hard to accomplish.

And yet it was. Marion sighed and rubbed her forehead. She didn't want to get out of her car. She didn't want to go into the building without Jess. At some point Jess and the building had become linked in her mind. She saw the building now and all she could think of were Jess's hands on her shoulders as she sipped unpleasant tea.

Marion fought back tears as she realized that Jess really was gone. This wasn't a fight where they would make up in a few days. She sat and stared ahead and just tried to breathe.

She startled badly when there was a tap on her window. With a gulp of air, Marion turned to see Gwen standing beside her car. She rolled her window down.

"Marion, dear, is everything all right? You've been sitting out here a good while." Gwen looked at her in concern.

"No, no. Everything's fine." But Marion couldn't get out of her car. As if sensing her dilemma, Gwen rounded the car and got in the passenger seat.

"Why don't you tell me what's really the matter." Gwen reached over and put her hand on Marion's knee, giving it a slight squeeze. Marion looked down at the hand on her knee. Tabitha might have been the reason for all of those early awards, but Gwen was the reason she had a career at all. Long, afternoon talks with Gwen in her trailer had given Marion an idea of the actress she wanted to be, had taught her how to fully embody a role. She had listened to Marion's troubles and passed her sweets that Tabitha had forbidden her. If there was anyone Marion could talk to, who would understand, it was Gwen.

"I think...I think I've done something horrible." She had driven Jess away and now that she was gone, Marion was full of regret and sorrow. It was over and she might never see Jess again. As Marion's first tears started to fall, she dashed them away with her hand.

"Does this have something to do with Jess?" Gwen asked gently. Marion took a shaky breath and nodded and truly started to cry.

"There, there, dear. It can't be as bad as all that. Why don't you tell me about it, and we'll see if we can't muddle through to a solution?" Gwen pulled out a handkerchief and offered it to Marion. It took her a few minutes to start, but then she told Gwen everything.

❖

2004

Marion turned on the radio then immediately turned it back off again. She took a deep breath then slowly turned the radio back on. She shouldn't. She knew she shouldn't. As soon as the volume was loud enough, Marion closed her eyes as Jess sang. It hurt. God, it hurt.

The words were about her. She knew that the words were about her, but she couldn't stop herself from listening. The song was everywhere. Even months after its release, it topped the charts. Marion couldn't escape it.

The Grammys had been a few nights before, and Marion had tried not to watch them. Somehow, her TV ended up on during the last hour, though she couldn't recall just how that happened. She had watched Jess perform, watched as the cameras zoomed in on her face as tears gathered at the edges of her eyes. The tears never fell, but it was a close thing. Jess had been captivating. Not just to Marion.

Jess had won, of course. She had won song of the year and album of the year. From what Marion could tell from the news coverage the next day, Jess had won every award she could. Marion couldn't escape her.

Marion forced herself to turn the radio off. She was supposed to be getting ready for another *date* with one of Tabitha's choice of partners for the moment. Who knew how long he would last. She couldn't fathom what exactly these men got out of dating her. It certainly wasn't sex. She supposed it must be recognition. Marion hated it. She turned her radio on again and just caught the end of Jess's song.

Marion knew she shouldn't listen, but she also knew that she would turn her radio on over and over again just to hear Jess's voice, just to feel close to her again.

She turned on the TV to distract herself, but that proved pointless. She just ended up aimlessly flicking through the channels.

A distinctive blond head suddenly appeared on Marion's screen. Marion stopped. MTV. That made sense, but Jess wasn't actually there. It was just a picture of her. Marion was ready to turn the channel when the presenter started speaking.

"And in other news, acclaimed musical icon Jess Carmichael held a press conference today announcing to the world that she's a proud member of the LGBT community."

Marion froze. Jess was out.

Marion didn't hear the rest of what the presenter said, but when he finished, Marion exhaled and felt pure relief.

If Jess was out, that meant it was over. All of it. Marion swallowed. Tabitha's threat was gone. Now that Jess was safe, she didn't care if Tabitha outed her. Maybe her career would survive. Maybe it wouldn't. Either way, she no longer cared. Jess was safe.

Ignoring the time, Marion picked up her phone and dialed a number she had long ago memorized. She waited for the call to connect. As soon as it did, she said the only thing she cared to say. "You're fired."

Marion practically threw the phone back into its cradle. She couldn't believe she had done it. She had actually fired Tabitha. She felt dizzy. She pressed a hand to her stomach and tried to catch her breath. Tabitha was gone.

She would have to find a new agent, one who wouldn't care that she was a lesbian, who wouldn't force her on dates with men just to maintain a reputation she didn't want.

Now it was over. Tabitha had loomed over her head for so long, terrified her for so long. Now, she was free.

❖

2011

Marion half smiled as another person congratulated her as she made her way to her dressing room. The potential to win an Olivier hadn't been why she had decided to take a break from Hollywood to return to London for a while, but it certainly didn't hurt. Now that the nominations were official though, it helped justify her decision.

"Way to go, Marion," Mark, one of the supporting actors, said as she passed him in the hallway just as she opened her door. She was there slightly earlier than she had to be, but she had a feeling everything was going to take a bit longer that evening. Even walking down the hallway had taken longer than usual.

Marion took a deep breath before she opened the door to her dressing room. Flowers. There were flowers everywhere, in every size and color imaginable. Stepping inside was like walking into a greenhouse. Every flat surface was covered, and several arrangements were sitting on the floor. She stepped carefully around them then started moving them off of her vanity where she would be able to get ready for the show that night.

It was while she was moving them that she saw the small bunch of violets. Her breath caught in her chest, and she let out a ragged exhale. Marion moved without thinking about it, lifting the flowers and searching for a card. She got the same bouquet at some point during every show she did, but there was never a card. She didn't know why she was looking for one now.

The hard cardboard stopped her short. She put the flowers down in favor of pulling the card from its envelope.

Congratulations.

It was scrawled in a vaguely familiar hand, but was most likely written by the florist who had taken the order over the phone. Marion tucked the card back in with the flowers. She decided then that she would take them home with her that night.

Mark poked his head into her dressing room just as she started removing her earrings. "VIPs in the audience tonight." That wasn't unusual. Now that the nominations had been announced, there would be plenty of nights when various famous people showed up to see the show. It didn't change anything, just meant that she'd have to spend more time at the theater than necessary shaking hands after her performance. "It's Jess Carmichael."

Marion's hands stuttered and she dropped her earring. "Damn." It felt like she had been punched in the stomach. She looked back at the flowers with wide eyes. Was that really possibly Jess's handwriting? How had Jess gotten so close without her realizing? Oh God, would Jess insist on coming backstage after the performance? Thoughts raced through Marion's brain while her hands unsuccessfully searched for her lost earring by rote.

"Do you need some help?" Mark asked.

If only there was someone or something that could help her with the feeling that her world had just been snatched out from under her. "No." She swallowed and finally looked up at Mark. "No, thank you."

Marion stepped to the center of the stage to take her bow. Somehow, she had managed to avoid spending the entire night looking for Jess in the audience, but now that the show was over, she found her eyes drawn magnetically to the box Jess was seated in. As soon as she found Jess, their eyes locked. Even from so far away, Marion could tell Jess was on the verge of tears. Was it because of the play, or something else? Someone next to Jess leaned over and whispered something in her ear and the effect was instantaneous. Their eye contact broke, and Jess turned and started laughing. It was only then that Marion recalled that she had heard Jess was dating someone. Josephine something-or-other. If the way they were smiling at each other meant anything, they seemed happy together. Marion wished it was her making Jess smile like that. But it wasn't. And it couldn't ever be. It was time to move on.

As soon as the curtain was down, Marion rushed backstage. She barely took the time to change out of her costume before she fled the theater. She didn't know if Jess and her date would want to come backstage, but Marion knew she couldn't be there if they did.

Chapter Sixteen

Present Day

Marion sat tiredly in her chair on the set of *Hallowed Hills*. It was only the middle of the afternoon, but they had started shooting at six in the morning, which meant getting to hair and makeup at five. It wasn't unusual, but it wasn't a joy either. She rubbed her forehead in an attempt to drive off some fatigue, but it wasn't working.

She watched as Lauren poured herself a cup of coffee and then took the seat next to Marion. Her smile was just as tired. Screenwriters didn't usually spend so much time on set, but the rewrites continued even though they had already started filming, and truthfully, it seemed like the director simply wanted her there as some sort of safety blanket.

Lauren shifted in her seat and furtively looked at Marion and then back at her coffee. The cycle repeated several times. Finally, Marion could take it no longer.

"Whatever it is, you're better off just telling me. What have you changed this time?" Despite the annoyance of the rewrites, the changes thus far had improved the story rather than detracting from it, so Marion chose to accept them with equanimity.

Lauren took a deep breath. "I didn't intend, I mean, it wasn't the point. We're not making—"

"Lauren." Marion tentatively reached out and placed a hand on Lauren's shoulder. It made Lauren jump, but it also seemed to relax her. She looked over at Marion with thanks in her eyes. "Just one word at a time. I promise I'm not going to yell at you or storm off the set."

Lauren nodded and swallowed as Marion removed her hand. "We want to make your character a lesbian. Not as the focus of the film, but there's a scene we want to add where she talks to her wife on the phone. We were originally going to have it be her husband, but it didn't feel right for the character. Or maybe it just didn't feel right for you? I mean, there's been this subtext in every film you've been in for the past decade, so maybe that's it."

Marion's eyes went wide but Lauren jumped in before she could say anything.

"I know you've never actually, technically played a lesbian, but we—I—just thought, if anyone was up for some surprise gayness, it would be you. I mean, if you hate it, we don't have to do the scene. But it seemed like a good idea?" Lauren's rambling finally stopped.

Marion put her hand back on Lauren's shoulder and squeezed it.

"Why do you think I'm here?"

"I don't...I don't understand." Marion looked at Lauren gently.

"Why do you think I'm here? It's certainly not because you can pay me. So clearly, I must be getting something out of it." Marion waited for Lauren to come up with an answer, but she just seemed lost. Marion took pity on her.

"I'm here because I believe in you, and I believe in your vision. Without that, I wouldn't be here. Without you, I don't have a character. If you think Agnes calls her wife, then she calls her wife. Write the scene and I'll play it. Do you understand?"

Lauren nodded. "Yeah." She exhaled as Marion let her go again. "Thanks. Thank you."

"You're welcome. Now, I think there's a young woman approaching us, and she must be here to see you because she certainly isn't here to see me." Marion nodded to a woman approaching Lauren from behind.

Lauren turned and lit up. She hopped up from her seat and met the other woman with two quick steps. Lauren wrapped her arms around the woman and pecked her on the lips. They had a short conversation before she took the woman's hand. Lauren tugged her forward shyly until they were by Marion's side again.

"Um…this is Safiyya. She's a composer. Jess introduced us at that party you guys threw." Lauren winced slightly at the mention of Jess, but she continued anyway. "She's my girlfriend and she really wanted to meet you. She didn't get a chance that night. Anyway, Safiyya, this is Marion Hargreaves." Lauren squeezed Safiyya's hand before she let it go so Marion and Safiyya could shake hands.

"It's lovely to meet you. Lauren is very talented, so I imagine you must be as well." Marion looked between them noticing how both were blushing and that they were holding hands once again.

"Thank you." Safiyya rubbed a hand over her cheek. "Can I just say, I think your work is amazing. The director has been letting me see some of the dailies where I can get started on my compositions, and the way you take up space on screen is just…wow. Yeah."

Marion swallowed. "That's very kind of you to say." It wasn't her first time getting such compliments, but they always surprised her.

"It must be a relief to get to actually play a queer character instead of just constantly hinting at it."

Marion raised her eyebrows. Clearly, Lauren and Safiyya had discussed the changes to the script already. "I told Lauren it was ridiculous for her to worry about asking a lesbian to play a lesbian, but…" Safiyya shrugged.

"Yes, well." Marion fought down a blush. "I'm looking forward to it."

"Babe." Lauren squeezed Safiyya's hand again. "We should probably leave Marion alone."

"Right." Safiyya smiled at Marion. "It was really awesome to meet you." She waved as Lauren drew her away.

Marion watched them go still holding hands as they walked toward the offices. It seemed so easy for them. Marion knew it took courage, but still, what would her life have been like if she and Jess could have walked around holding hands without worrying about losing their careers, without losing everything.

Marion looked down at her hands. But she and Jess could have that now, couldn't they? It was only Marion who was keeping them from walking around holding hands. Wasn't that what Jess had said she wanted? To hold her hand, to go out with her, to just live their lives together. And Marion had said no. God, she was an idiot. Jess was on the other side of the country and she was an idiot. Marion buried her face in her hands. Was it too late?

❖

Lauren knocked on the door to Marion's trailer and opened it without waiting for any acknowledgement. It had been a long day and Marion was already half asleep. She was tempted to just spend the night on the couch in her trailer, but she wasn't quite that far gone yet. She looked up at Lauren as she slid through the door.

"Yes?" Marion didn't have the energy to be more polite than that.

"I just wanted to see if you were okay." Lauren closed the door behind herself.

"Why wouldn't I be okay?" Marion rubbed her temple with one hand as she looked up at Lauren from her seat on the couch.

Lauren shrugged. "I don't know. It just seems like you've spent most of the day brooding. I know if I had done that, you'd have checked on me, so I thought, you know." She carefully sat next to Marion.

"Thank you, but I'm fine." Marion wouldn't let her problems become Lauren's. She was fine. She would be fine.

"Is it about Jess? I figured out you guys broke up or something when she told me she was going to New York for a few months. But you haven't, well, you haven't seemed quite this depressed before. I mean, you're an excellent actress, so I guess if you didn't want anyone to know how you were feeling, you'd be really good at hiding it. But you just seem off today. I dunno." Lauren twisted her fingers together as she waited for Marion to say something.

Marion carefully considered her next words. "You've spoken to Jess?" She couldn't help herself. She needed to know how Jess was, what she was doing. She knew it wasn't her place anymore, but she couldn't let it go.

"Yeah. Not much. Only a couple of times. She's, um, yeah…" Lauren seemed reluctant to share more and Marion wouldn't press. "She's hosting SNL tomorrow night," Lauren volunteered.

"That's…that's good, I suppose." Marion closed her eyes. She didn't want to think about Jess being so far away, so far out of reach.

"Can I ask what happened?" Lauren said tentatively.

Marion waved a hand. "She wanted our relationship to be more public than I did." It sounded ridiculous when she said it out loud. She knew it wasn't only that.

"Oh." Lauren looked like she was thinking hard about something. "I guess it's hard to be in the closet and date Jess Carmichael at the same time."

"Exceedingly." Marion closed her eyes. Maybe it was worth it, though.

Lauren nodded. "You know no one would care, right? I mean, not anyone important. Yeah, the tabloids would talk about it for a few days, but it's not the nineties. It wouldn't be a big story. I mean, it's Jess, and she has a lot of fans, and you're you and you never tell anyone anything, so yeah, people would pay attention for a while, but you'd be like this awesome lesbian power couple. People would swoon. It wouldn't be bad." She carefully took Marion's hand and squeezed it.

"Wouldn't it?" Marion looked at Lauren tiredly. "I'm forty-seven. I've been hiding this since I was fifteen. I don't know if I know how to stop."

"Do you want to stop?" Lauren asked gently.

Marion rested her head against her fingertips and sighed deeply. "I don't know. It was my first agent. I was so dependent on her." Marion shook her head and sat up. She swallowed. "She hated me. I couldn't see it then, but I truly think she hated me. She made it seem like it would be a disaster if anyone ever found out. She burrowed herself into every corner of my life. If I did the slightest thing she didn't approve of, there would be consequences. I was afraid of losing her, of losing my success, of losing the only thing that anyone ever valued about me. But this was something she couldn't control about me, couldn't change. By the end, all I wanted was to be left alone. After I finally fired her, God, I just wanted to have control over my own life. And not to worry what *anyone* thought about me."

Lauren nodded in sympathy. "And that's why you didn't want to tell everyone about you and Jess?"

"Is it too much to ask just to be left alone?" Marion shook her head. "Gwen apologized to me the other day. Said she was sorry that she hadn't been able to support me when I needed it. As if Tabitha would have let her."

"Tabitha sounds like a bitch."

Marion caught herself off guard with her own laughter. "That is exactly what she was."

"You know, if you told all of that to Jess, she might understand." Lauren squeezed Marion's hand again.

"Even if that were true, Jess would never take me back. I've hurt her too much, too many times." Marion closed her eyes. There was no path she could see to Jess forgiving her again.

"I think you're wrong." Lauren squeezed Marion's hand again. "I think she loves you as much as you love her and that she's in as much pain as you are right now. And I dunno, I'm a romantic. I think if you love her, you should stop wallowing and go try to get her back."

"If only it was so easy." Marion closed her eyes. She was so tired. She just wanted Jess to be there, she wanted to be able to go home to her, to pull her into her arms and curl up with her at night.

"It's only complicated if you make it complicated." Lauren stood up and got ready to leave. "If you're asking me, I think you should go get your girl."

CHAPTER SEVENTEEN

Present Day

She was an idiot.

She loved Jess. She loved her. None of the rest mattered. None of it. It didn't matter that there would be gossip and that her precious, precious privacy would be gone. She needed Jess. She couldn't go back to missing her for twenty years.

She picked up her phone, thumb hovering over Jess's number to call her. No. That wouldn't be enough. Jess had said words wouldn't be enough anymore, that she needed to be a part of Marion's life, that she wouldn't wait for Marion to be ready. Well, Marion was ready now. She just hoped it wasn't too late.

She would be cutting it close, but if she could catch a flight to New York soon, she could make it before the episode of *Saturday Night Live* Jess was hosting started. Suddenly, it had become very important that she see Jess before Jess had a chance to go on stage.

It was late enough that she felt guilty calling her assistant, but Barbara had a way of making things happen that Marion couldn't explain. Marion picked up her phone to make the call.

"Marion?" Barbara picked up the phone. "What's wrong? Are you in the hospital? Is someone dead?"

Marion ignored both questions. "I need to be on the next flight to New York. Kennedy, La Guardia, wherever. It doesn't matter how much it costs. Just get me there."

"All right. Give me a little time and I'll call you back, okay?"

Marion huffed in impatience. "Fine. As soon as you can." Marion didn't wait for Barbara to hang up. She tapped the end icon on her phone. She needed to get home. She needed to pack.

❖

The area backstage in Studio 8H was a warren of rooms and corridors. With only a few minutes to air, people rushed around in a frenzy. A few people did double takes when they saw her hunting through the hallways, but they were used to random celebrities showing up at the last minute. It was entirely possible she had a cameo in a sketch, and no one had told them. It wouldn't be the first time. No one accosted her, but it meant she had to get someone's attention to give her directions, and that was surprisingly difficult.

Finally, she found one of the crew members and stopped her. "Jess Carmichael's dressing room?"

"Two lefts and a right." The crewmember motioned with her head before she disappeared behind the stage.

Marion followed her directions as best she could and finally found a room with a star on the door and Jess's name written in dry erase marker. Marion took a moment to compose herself. After this, she couldn't go back.

She knocked on the door and waited for a muffled *come in*. It never came. Marion tried the handle and the door opened easily enough, but when she leaned into the room it was empty.

Marion looked around frantically grabbing the arm of someone walking past. "Where's Jess?"

She must have looked as unsettled as she felt. The man looked at her twice before he nodded back the way Marion had come. "Stage right."

Marion nodded and ran back the way she had come. She had minutes, maybe even seconds before Jess had to go on stage and Marion needed to talk to her first.

Finally, she found her way back to the stage. Jess. She needed to find Jess. She looked around desperately until she laid eyes on her. A few big strides had her close enough to reach out, but before she could get there, Jess turned and looked at Marion in surprise. "Marion, what are you doing here?" Her words nearly got swallowed up by the general din of everything going on around them.

"I love you." Marion took a shallow breath.

"What?" Jess shook her head. "I can't hear you."

Marion took a deep breath. "I love you," she shouted over all of the noise around them. Suddenly everything was quiet.

"What—?" Jess reeled back. "Marion?"

"I love you. I have always loved you and I will always love you and I don't care who knows. We can take out a sign in Times Square if you want, but I can't spend another day without you." Their eyes locked together.

"You wanted to know if I was serious. I'm serious. I'm here and I have never been so serious about something in my life," Marion said with conviction. "If you want me to be here to catch you, I will always be here." Marion's chest heaved and her heart beat in double time as she waited for Jess to say something.

"Marion—"

"Jess Carmichael to the stage. Jess Carmichael to the stage," rang through the PA system. Jess growled in frustration.

"I have to go. You just stay here. If you aren't here when I finish—" Jess pursed her lips. However Jess wanted to finish that threat, she didn't get the chance as her name was called out again and a stagehand came over. The noise level picked up again.

With one last look back, Jess stepped onto the stage.

❖

After the monologue, Marion watched the show from just beside one of the cameras, forced to move from the wings by the crew. But Jess would know where she was. She would be able to see her the entire time. Jess had looked dazed until the last second before her monologue started but suddenly snapped into focus as they counted her in. She kept things funny and light, and as she always did, she left the studio audience charmed. She left Marion in awe.

Marion paced as much as she could in the small space. It felt like she was in purgatory as she waited for the hour and a half to come to an end. Sketch after sketch passed without her attention. What had Jess wanted to say? After ninety minutes to think about it, what would Jess say when the show ended?

Finally, it was over. The cast devolved into a party on stage, dancing around as the cameras faded out, but even before that could happen, Jess was pushing her way through the crowd. Marion waited with bated breath as Jess got closer.

Without warning, Jess broke into a run and threw herself at Marion, arms around her neck and legs around her waist. Marion staggered back and nearly tripped over the camera before righting them both. Somewhere a laugh rang out.

"If you ever do something like this to me again, I will murder you." Before Marion could respond, Jess pressed their lips together as hard as she could and pulled Marion down into a deep, searching kiss. Marion's mind reeled. She grasped at Jess's waist and held on for dear life. She couldn't afford to drop Jess. Their lips were swollen and bruised by the time the kiss finally ended and they pulled apart, though neither of them went far.

"You'd really take out a billboard in Times Square?" Jess whispered.

"If that's what you want." Marion brushed her nose against Jess's cheek.

"Why don't we start with the afterparty and go from there?" Jess kissed Marion once again.

"You mean I can't just take you back to your hotel room?" Marion frowned.

"I have to go to the party. It's only polite. And if I have to go, you have to go because I'm not letting you out of my sight any time soon." Jess buried her face into Marion's shoulder and finally let her legs fall back to the floor. Marion kissed the side of her head. "In case it wasn't obvious, I love you too. The past month has been horrible. I missed you so much."

"I missed you too." Marion somehow pulled Jess even closer. "I thought about you every day until I just couldn't bear it anymore. I wasn't going to spend another twenty years pining for you."

"I'm glad you're here, but I need to take my makeup off now and get changed so we can go to this damned party." Jess slowly extracted herself from Marion's arms.

"Do you want me to wait here?"

"Not a chance in hell." Jess squeezed Marion's hand. "I meant what I said about not letting you out of my sight. We'll just have to control ourselves for ten minutes."

"If that's what you want." Marion would do anything Jess wanted without question.

The party had been interminably long, but they were finally in the elevator on the way to Jess's room. Jess hadn't let her get more than an arm's length away all night. They had touched constantly, hands on elbows and backs and waists. They'd stopped only long enough to drink the champagne a cast member had bought to toast to their renewed relationship. The champagne was gone along with the crowds, and they were alone. Jess laced their fingers together and looked at Marion through the side of her eye, a grin overtaking her face.

"You really jumped on a plane and flew across the country to tell me you loved me." Jess swayed closer and held onto Marion's hand harder.

"I did." Marion blushed.

"You know I'll be back in LA in a few days, right?" Jess couldn't keep the smug amusement out of her eyes.

"It seemed very important that I tell you as soon as possible." Marion looked down at their joined hands.

Jess moved until she was standing in front of Marion. She reached up and cupped the sides of Marion's face. "It was incredibly romantic." She leaned in and kissed Marion lightly. She stepped closer and wrapped her arms around Marion, resting her forehead on Marion's shoulder. "I hope you know you're not getting any sleep tonight."

Marion laughed as the elevator door opened. "Let's at least get into your room first."

"If you insist." Jess led Marion down the hallway to her room and opened the door. As soon as they were through it, Jess pressed herself up against Marion and covered her mouth with her own. Marion curled her fingers into Jess's waist and held her close as they kissed.

"I'm also going to insist we find your bed. I don't think I'm capable of sex against a door anymore."

Jess laughed between the kisses she left on Marion's neck. "I think you're wrong, but I'm not opposed to not ending up on my back on the floor." She stepped back and grabbed Marion's hand again, pulling her through the suite and into the bedroom.

❖

Marion gasped as she felt how wet Jess was under her fingers. She pushed one, then two, inside her—thrusting in and then pulling out. "Jess!" They were finally here, completely and fully. Jess was naked beneath her, skin pressed to skin as they moved against each other.

Jess clutched at Marion's shoulders as she arched up into Marion's touch, moving her hips in rhythm with Marion's thrusts. Each moment brought her closer to the edge and Marion could feel the tension building in her body.

"God, Marion," Jess moaned. She cupped Marion's face with her hands and drew her into a kiss. She wrapped her legs around Marion's waist. "Please. Please." She pulled Marion closer and closer and closer until there was no space left between them.

"I love you. God, I love you." Jess tossed her head as they moved together. Marion couldn't believe they were here, together, and she wasn't going to let Jess go again any time soon.

Sweat shone on their bodies as the air in the room got hotter and hotter. The blankets were already strewn on the floor. Marion had already made Jess come once. She could still taste her on her mouth, but she needed to be inside Jess, fingers as deep as they could go.

They kept rocking against each other as Marion brought her thumb around to touch Jess's clit. She still remembered how to touch Jess. She was sure she'd never forget. She circled Jess's clit in time with her thrusts.

"Please," Jess whimpered again as she pushed her hips up.

"I've got you, Jess. I've got you." Marion whispered as she kissed Jess's neck. She gasped as Jess's nails scratched over her shoulders. Marion bent her fingers forward and slid her thumb along the side of Jess's clit just the way Jess liked and then Jess curled into her, muscles tightening, clenching and unclenching as Jess came around her fingers.

Marion kissed Jess through the aftermath, gently helping her down until she calmed again. As Marion removed her fingers, Jess started laughing. She wrapped her arms around Marion again.

"I love you," Jess said. "I love you so much."

❖

Marion hummed in contentment. It was nearing sunrise as they lay in bed entwined in each other. Jess played with Marion's hand turning it over to trace the lines of her palm then back over to trace the tendons on the back. She brought Marion's hand up to kiss her fingertips. Sated for the moment, neither of them was willing to part from the other long enough to go to sleep.

"Have there…this is going to make me sound jealous and I promise I'm not, but have there been others?" Jess looked up at Marion from where she was settled on her shoulder.

"A few. Not many." Marion shrugged. There was no use in pretending otherwise. "None of them were you though."

"All of those men they said you were dating?" Jess trailed her fingers down between Marion's breasts to her stomach where she splayed out her hand.

"A cover, but there were women. Very discreetly. More after Margaret became my agent, but never anything serious."

Jess nodded.

"You dated, oh, what was her name?" Marion remembered seeing them together at the play. She remembered how happy Jess had looked.

"Mm-hmm, Josephine." Jess snuggled closer.

"Right. You dated her for a few years, didn't you? Was it serious?" Marion kissed the top of Jess's head as she pulled her a little closer.

Jess shrugged. "As serious as it could be when I was still hung up on someone else."

"Jess, I'm sorry." They hadn't really talked about the past yet, about what had happened. About Berlin and everything that came after. It hurt Marion to know that Jess hadn't been as happy as she could have been and that it had been Marion's fault.

"No. It's fine. I promise." Even though they were already skin to skin, Jess pulled Marion closer.

"The violets." Marion ran her fingers over Jess's ribs where the flowers in question were inked on her skin. "Every play I ever appeared in, halfway through the run, I'd get a bouquet of violets."

Jess blushed and looked away. "Are you asking if I sent them?"

"No. I always knew it was you." Marion cupped Jess's face and turned it toward her. She leaned in and placed a light kiss on Jess's lips. "It made it very hard to forget about you."

"Is that what you wanted? To forget about me?"

"Yes," Marion said softly. "And no. I tried. I tried for fifteen years. I could almost get there, but then one of your songs would come on the radio or I'd see you in a tabloid at the grocery store. And there were the violets."

"I'm sorry I made things more difficult." Jess sounded contrite. Marion kissed her lightly to silence her.

"By succeeding? By being a star? Don't wish away those things on my account. If I had really wanted to forget, I could have. But I didn't. Not really."

Jess nodded. She snuggled into Marion's shoulder. "I wrote about you. Every song on *Longing* was about you. And on *Revelations*. On all of them, really. It was the only way I knew…"

Marion sucked in a breath.

"It was Tabitha." She said it before she knew what she was saying, the name just tumbled out.

"Your old agent? What does she have to do with anything?"

Marion took another deep breath. She had never wanted Jess to find out why it had ended. She knew that Jess would blame herself, but a revelation for a revelation. Wasn't that a lyric in one of Jess's songs? "She found out about us. She had me followed."

Jess lifted her head from Marion's shoulder and looked down at her, curiosity written on her face. Marion couldn't meet her eyes. "She threatened to out you. That's why I didn't come to Germany. She said if I went, she would tell the world. She couldn't do anything to me, it would have destroyed her career too, but you…" Marion shook her head. "It was 1997. You weren't touring with Lilith Fair. It would have destroyed your career. I couldn't make that choice for you. You came out a decade later and there was still backlash, still people calling for boycotts of your music."

Jess's eyes went wide as she stared at Marion. Marion stared back, searching for Jess's thoughts.

"Marion. Oh, *Marion*." Tears welled in Jess's eyes, but she blinked them away.

"You know," Jess chuckled through her tears, "I always wanted to play Lilith Fair. I could never convince my management it was a good idea. *Not your sort of music*, they said."

"Jess, this isn't…"

"Shh, I know." Jess kissed her lightly and settled again. Marion could tell that her mind was still reeling. "You got rid of Tabitha."

"After you came out. She lost her leverage. She wanted me to marry Christopher, but then you came out, and I was so tired of the threats. I just couldn't anymore. If she had outed me then I wouldn't have cared." Marion sighed and shook her head. "But she didn't. She just retired."

Jess splayed out her hand over Marion's stomach. "If I had known—"

"It wouldn't have changed anything. Neither of us could afford to be out then, but you would have wanted to do it anyway just to protect me. I couldn't let you." Marion looked intently at Jess. Jess's breath caught in her throat.

"You're right." Jess swallowed. "I would have done it in a heartbeat. If it had meant we could have been together."

"We couldn't have." Jess looked away again. "I loved you, but that love wouldn't have been enough. Not then. We both wanted too much. We would have constantly been looking over our shoulders. We never would have been able to tell anyone. In the long run, it wouldn't have been enough."

"And now it is," Jess said.

"Now it is."

EPILOGUE

Marion slid out of the car and turned to help Jess. Jess smiled brilliantly up at her in the afternoon light. The red carpet, the Academy Awards. Despite the fact that Marion had become a regular feature of Jess's Instagram account and that they were now often photographed together by the paparazzi, it was the first time they were seriously appearing together in public. After tonight, there would be no doubt in anyone's mind that they were together. They already had an interview lined up with *Rolling Stone* to appear in a few weeks.

Jess didn't show it, but Marion could feel her nerves by the way her hand lightly shook as Marion clasped it in her own. She gave it a brief squeeze as they took their first steps down the red carpet. With every step they took, the screams of the crowd grew louder. People really did love Jess in a way that Marion couldn't fathom, in a way Marion had never experienced, but she didn't begrudge Jess the adoration. After all, she adored Jess too, if in a more personal way.

Jess's work on *Petunia's Potion* had earned her what Marion thought was a well-deserved nomination for best original song. But the red carpet was a gauntlet they had to survive to get there. She lifted Jess's hand to place a spontaneous kiss against the back of her fingers. A flurry of flashbulbs caught the movement and Marion wondered how many blogs would feature that moment the next day, or even that night before the ceremony ended.

Jess looked at Marion wide eyed for a second before her expression melted into something softer, something calmer. Marion knew her plan had worked when Jess let out a long breath. Marion smiled a small, private smile and Jess returned it.

A few steps later and they were at the dais where the MC for the preshow was interviewing passing celebrities. Marion helped Jess up the steps, straightening out the train of Jess's pink confection of a dress behind her before she did her best to fade into the background. This was Jess's night, and Marion didn't want to insert herself into it.

She tuned out what they were talking about, but she did notice when Jess looked over to her. She kept her face as pleasantly neutral as possible while she was sure the camera was focused on her. Then Jess was looking at her pleadingly and holding her hand out. Marion sighed and climbed the dais herself.

Jess reached out and twined their fingers together again.

"Marion, it's good to see you again." There was glee in the MC's eyes as he said it. "I wasn't sure we'd be able to get you up here on camera."

"I'm always happy to make an appearance." It was a blatant lie but nobody watching knew it. "But why don't we skip to what you actually want to know?"

"You and Jess showed up here together. Is this a confirmation of one of the biggest current rumors in

Hollywood?" He was bouncing on his toes at the chance for an exclusive.

Repressing her annoyance, Marion smiled over at Jess, checking to make sure she was okay with what Marion was about to say. She got a small nod of encouragement and that was enough.

"I'm sure everyone knows I keep my personal life quite private, so I will say this once. You'd best have your microphones ready." Marion paused to give them a chance to make sure the camera was in focus and the microphones were, in fact, on. "Jess Carmichael is the love of my life, and she has been for some time. Make of that what you will, but I won't be discussing our relationship beyond saying that we are both very happy."

She immediately looked back at Jess once she finished and found Jess beaming at her.

"Well, you heard it here first, folks," The MC turned toward the camera, playing it up. Marion turned to Jess.

"I'll be waiting when you're finished," she whispered, and disappeared back down the stairs before the MC could turn back around.

Jess put on her most charming persona and chatted with him for a few more moments, likely about her dress, before she handed the microphone back to an assistant and came back down the stairs. Marion took Jess's hand again.

"God, I hope I didn't sound like an idiot," Jess whispered in a rare moment of public doubt. Her hands shook again.

"You were perfect." Marion pulled Jess closer.

Jess laughed before she leaned in and pressed her forehead to the outside of Marion's shoulder. "The love of your life, hmm?"

"You already knew that." Marion smiled.

"Yes, but a girl never gets tired of hearing it. If we didn't have somewhere else to be, I'd take you back home right now."

Marion chuckled and hoped that none of the microphones picked that up. Then, she ushered Jess forward and into the theater, leading them to their front row seats.

❖

Marion's stomach fluttered as the lights rose on Jess. Even though Marion knew Jess had performed in front of millions of people at thousands of concerts, even though Marion knew Jess had performed at the Oscars before, this felt different. It felt like the entire last year had built to this night. She wondered if Jess felt the same.

Jess had changed for the performance, something shorter and easier to move in. The song was too upbeat for her to stay in one place while she sang. That wasn't really Jess's style anyway.

The band started to play, and Jess came in right on cue. The movie stars in the audience gamely clapped along and laughed when Jess came down off of the stage during the musical break and walked down in front of the first row soliciting high fives. She stopped when she got to Marion. For a second, she looked like she was going to pull Marion up to dance with her, but Marion's panic must have shown on her face and stopped her because instead she just winked and headed back up the stairs to the stage to continue singing.

Marion barely had time to catch her breath before Jess finished the song, the audience started clapping, and the broadcast went to commercial. Before the commercial break ended, Jess returned to her seat by Marion's side.

"You were terrified I was about to make you dance on national TV, weren't you?" Jess teased her, before leaning in and kissing Marion's cheek then immediately wiping away even the traces of evidence she had done it.

"I was concerned." Marion tried not to let on that she was breathing a little faster than normal. Seeing Jess's performances just did that to her.

"Don't worry, I'm saving that for the Grammys in a few weeks." Jess threaded her fingers between Marion's and settled. It seemed that with her performance finished, Jess had set aside her earlier nerves.

"I think I might be coming down with something," Marion said. The dimming of the lights cut off any retort Jess might have been contemplating.

❖

Jess's grip on Marion's hand got tighter and tighter as the announcer read out the nominees for Best Original Song. Marion was sure Jess was going to break her hand as the presenter opened the envelope.

"And the Oscar goes to—" The presenter paused. Marion felt Jess stop breathing. "Jess Carmichael for *Petunia's Potion*."

Jess suddenly started breathing again. "Did he just…?" Jess looked at Marion in wide eyed shock. She seemed completely dazed.

"You need to go up there." Marion lifted Jess's hand to prompt her to stand. Jess started shaking again, but Marion helped her to her feet. Jess swallowed and took several deep breaths before she could climb the stairs, but she made it up them and only fumbled a little when she took the statuette into her hands. She looked down at it as if she wasn't sure it was real before she looked back up at the audience. Marion smiled up at her, silently encouraging her to start her speech.

"I have to thank—God, I have so many people to thank. Felidae Studios for taking a chance on me and letting me put my mark on this amazing film, and of course all of the actors. Everyone on the film who made this the most extraordinary experience. And, oh, Marion, I love you so much. So much. I can't even...I...this..." Jess motioned with her Oscar. "This is *ours*." Marion could see Jess fighting back tears. "You have been my muse and my inspiration for more than half of my life and I absolutely would not be here without you. Thank you. *Thank you*."

Marion didn't hear anything after that, just a chuckle from the audience and some more clapping. She knew the cameras were on her once again and she couldn't school her features. She was much too proud of Jess to do that. She knew she was smiling like an idiot, she knew she was blushing, but she couldn't bring herself to stop. The moment was perfect, and she sat in it waiting for Jess to return.

End

About the Author

Ashley Moore is a paralegal living in Charleston, South Carolina, with her dog, Tallulah. She went to college in Georgia, law school in Virginia, and has lived in seven states in the last fifteen years. Her interests include craft cocktails and woodworking. You can find her at her website: AshleyMooreWrites.com and on Twitter @AMWrites.

Books Available from Bold Strokes Books

A Different Man by Andrew L. Huerta. This diverse collection of stories chronicling the challenges of gay life at various ages shines a light on the progress made and the progress still to come. (978-1-63555-977-4)

All That Remains by Sheri Lewis Wohl. Johnnie and Shantel might have to risk their lives—and their love—to stop a werewolf intent on killing. (978-1-63555-949-1)

Beginner's Bet by Fiona Riley. Phenom luxury Realtor Ellison Gamble has everything, except a family to share it with, so when a mix-up brings youthful Katie Crawford into her life, she bets the house on love. (978-1-63555-733-6)

Dangerous Without You by Lexus Grey. Throughout their senior year in high school, Aspen, Remington, Denna, and Raleigh face challenges in life and romance that they never expect. (978-1-63555-947-7)

Desiring More by Raven Sky. In this collection of steamy stories, a rich variety of lovers find themselves desiring more, more from a lover, more from themselves, and more from life. (978-1-63679-037-4)

Jordan's Kiss by Nanisi Barrett D'Arnuck. After losing everything in a fire, Jordan Phelps joins a small lounge band and meets pianist Morgan Sparks, who lights another blaze, this time in Jordan's heart. (978-1-63555-980-4)

Late City Summer by Jeanette Bears. Forced together for her wedding, Emily Stanton and Kate Alessi navigate their lingering passion for one another against the backdrop of New York City and World War II, and a summer romance they left behind. (978-1-63555-968-2)

Love and Lotus Blossoms by Anne Shade. On her path to self-acceptance and true passion, Janesse will risk everything—and possibly everyone—she loves. (978-1-63555-985-9)

Love in the Limelight by Ashley Moore. Marion Hargreaves, the finest actress of her generation, and Jessica Carmichael, the world's biggest pop star, rediscover each other twenty years after an ill-fated affair. (978-1-63679-051-0)

Suspecting Her by Mary P. Burns. Complications ensue when Erin O'Connor falls for top real estate saleswoman Catherine Williams while investigating racism in the real estate industry; the fallout could end their chance at happiness. (978-1-63555-960-6)

Two Winters by Lauren Emily Whalen. A modern YA retelling of Shakespeare's *The Winter's Tale* about birth, death, Catholic school, improv comedy, and the healing nature of time. (978-1-63679-019-0)

Busy Ain't the Half of It by Frederick Smith and Chaz Lamar Cruz. Elijah and Justin seek happily-ever-afters in LA, but are they too busy to notice happiness when it's there? (978-1-63555-944-6)

Calumet by Ali Vali. Jaxon Lavigne and Iris Long had a forbidden small-town romance that didn't last, and the consequences of that love will be uncovered fifteen years later at their high school reunion. (978-1-63555-900-2)

Her Countess to Cherish by Jane Walsh. London Society's material girl realizes there is more to life than diamonds when she falls in love with a non-binary bluestocking. (978-1-63555-902-6)

Hot Days, Heated Nights by Renee Roman. When Cole and Lee meet, instant attraction quickly flares into uncontrollable passion, but their connection might be short lived as Lee's identity is tied to her life in the city. (978-1-63555-888-3)

Never Be the Same by MA Binfield. Casey meets Olivia and sparks fly in this opposites attract romance that proves love can be found in the unlikeliest places. (978-1-63555-938-5)

Quiet Village by Eden Darry. Something not quite human is stalking Collie and her niece, and she'll be forced to work with undercover reporter Emily Lassiter if they want to get out of Hyam alive. (978-1-63555-898-2)

Shaken or Stirred by Georgia Beers. Bar owner Julia Martini and home health aide Savannah McNally attempt to weather the storms brought on by a mysterious blogger trashing the bar, family feuds they knew nothing about, and way too much advice from way too many relatives. (978-1-63555-928-6)

The Fiend in the Fog by Jess Faraday. Can four people on different trajectories work together to save the vulnerable residents of East London from the terrifying fiend in the fog before it's too late? (978-1-63555-514-1)

The Marriage Masquerade by Toni Logan. A no strings attached marriage scheme to inherit a Maui B&B uncovers unexpected attractions and a dark family secret. (978-1-63555-914-9)

Flight SQA016 by Amanda Radley. Fastidious airline passenger Olivia Lewis is used to things being a certain way. When her routine is changed by a new, attractive member of the staff, sparks fly. (978-1-63679-045-9)

Home Is Where the Heart Is by Jenny Frame. Can Archie make the countryside her home and give Ash the fairytale romance she desires? Or will the countryside and small village life all be too much for her? (978-1-63555-922-4)

Moving Forward by PJ Trebelhorn. The last person Shelby Ryan expects to be attracted to is Iris Calhoun, the sister of the man who killed her wife four years and three thousand miles ago. (978-1-63555-953-8)

Poison Pen by Jean Copeland. Debut author Kendra Blake is finally living her best life until a nasty book review and exposed secrets threaten her promising new romance with aspiring journalist Alison Chatterley. (978-1-63555-849-4)

Seasons for Change by KC Richardson. Love, laughter, and trust develop for Shawn and Morgan throughout the changing seasons of Lake Tahoe. (978-1-63555-882-1)

Summer Lovin' by Julie Cannon. Three different women, three exotic locations, one unforgettable summer. What do you think will happen? (978-1-63555-920-0)

Unbridled by D. Jackson Leigh. A visit to a local stable turns into more than riding lessons between a novel writer and an equestrian with a taste for power play. (978-1-63555-847-0)

VIP by Jackie D. In a town where relationships are forged and shattered by perception, sometimes even love can't change who you really are. (978-1-63555-908-8)

Yearning by Gun Brooke. The sleepy town of Dennamore has an irresistible pull on those who've moved away. The mystery Darian Benson and Samantha Pike uncover will change them forever, but the love they find along the way just might be the key to saving themselves. (978-1-63555-757-2)

A Turn of Fate by Ronica Black. Will Nev and Kinsley finally face their painful past and relent to their powerful, forbidden attraction? Or will facing their past be too much to fight through? (978-1-63555-930-9)

Desires After Dark by MJ Williamz. When her human lover falls deathly ill, Alex, a vampire, must decide which is worse, letting her go or condemning her to everlasting life. (978-1-63555-940-8)

Her Consigliere by Carsen Taite. FBI agent Royal Scott swore an oath to uphold the law, and criminal defense attorney Siobhan Collins pledged her loyalty to the only family she's ever known, but will their love be stronger than the bonds they've vowed to others, or will their competing allegiances tear them apart? (978-1-63555-924-8)

In Our Words: Queer Stories from Black, Indigenous, and People of Color Writers. Stories selected by Anne Shade and edited by Victoria Villaseñor. Comprising both the renowned and emerging voices of Black, Indigenous, and People of Color authors, this thoughtfully curated collection of short stories explores the intersection of racial and queer identity. (978-1-63555-936-1)

Measure of Devotion by CF Frizzell. Disguised as her late twin brother, Catherine Samson enters the Civil War to defend the Constitution as a Union soldier, never expecting her life to be altered by a Gettysburg farmer's daughter. (978-1-63555-951-4)

Not Guilty by Brit Ryder. Claire Weaver and Emery Pearson's day jobs clash, even as their desire for each other burns, and a discreet sex-only arrangement is the only option. (978-1-63555-896-8)

Opposites Attract: Butch/Femme Romances by Meghan O'Brien, Aurora Rey, Angie Williams. Sometimes opposites really do attract. Fall in love with these butch/femme romance novellas. (978-1-63555-784-8)

Swift Vengeance by Jean Copeland, Jackie D, Erin Zak. A journalist becomes the subject of her own investigation when sudden strange, violent visions summon her to a summer retreat and into the arms of a killer's possible next victim. (978-1-63555-880-7)

Under Her Influence by Amanda Radley. On their path to #truelove, will Beth and Jemma discover that reality is even better than illusion? (978-1-63555-963-7)

Wasteland by Kristin Keppler & Allisa Bahney. Danielle Clark is fighting against the National Armed Forces and finds peace as a scavenger, until the NAF general's daughter, Katelyn Turner, shows up on her doorstep and brings the fight right back to her. (978-1-63555-935-4)

When in Doubt by VK Powell. Police officer Jeri Wylder thinks she committed a crime in the line of duty but can't remember, until details emerge pointing to a cover-up by those close to her. (978-1-63555-955-2)

A Woman to Treasure by Ali Vali. An ancient scroll isn't the only treasure Levi Montbard finds as she starts her hunt for the truth—all she has to do is prove to Yasmine Hassani that there's more to her than an adventurous soul. (978-1-63555-890-6)

Before. After. Always. by Morgan Lee Miller. Still reeling from her tragic past, Eliza Walsh has sworn off taking risks, until Blake Navarro turns her world right-side up, making her question if falling in love again is worth it. (978-1-63555-845-6)

Bet the Farm by Fiona Riley. Lauren Calloway's luxury real estate sale of the century comes to a screeching halt when dairy farm heiress, and one-night stand, Thea Boudreaux calls her bluff. (978-1-63555-731-2)

Cowgirl by Nance Sparks. The last thing Aren expects is to fall for Carol. Sharing her home is one thing, but sharing her heart means sharing the demons in her past and risking everything to keep Carol safe. (978-1-63555-877-7)

Give In to Me by Elle Spencer. Gabriela Talbot never expected to sleep with her favorite author—certainly not after the scathing review she'd given Whitney Ainsworth's latest book. (978-1-63555-910-1)

Hidden Dreams by Shelley Thrasher. A lethal virus and its resulting vision send Texan Barbara Allan and her lovely guide, Dara, on a journey up Cambodia's Mekong River in search of Barbara's mother's mystifying past. (978-1-63555-856-2)

In the Spotlight by Lesley Davis. For actresses Cole Calder and Eris Whyte, their chance at love runs out fast when a fan's adoration turns to obsession. (978-1-63555-926-2)

Origins by Jen Jensen. Jamis Bachman is pulled into a dangerous mystery that becomes personal when she learns the truth of her origins as a ghost hunter. (978-1-63555-837-1)

Pursuit: A Victorian Entertainment by Felice Picano. An intelligent, handsome, ruthlessly ambitious young man who rose from the slums to become the right-hand man of the Lord Exchequer of England will stop at nothing as he pursues his Lord's vanished wife across Continental Europe. (978-1-63555-870-8)

Unrivaled by Radclyffe. Zoey Cohen will never accept second place in matters of the heart, even when her rival is a career, and Declan Black has nothing left to give of herself or her heart. (978-1-63679-013-8)